J BARRON
Barron, T. A.
Giant.

 **W9-BZC-004**

DEC 0 6 2021

WITHDRAWN

PREQUEL TO THE

SAGA

THE MERLIN SAGA

PREQUEL TO THE

MERLIN

SAGA

GIANT

T. A. BARRON

Philomel Books

PHILOMEL BOOKS

An imprint of Penguin Random House LLC, New York

First published in the United States of America by Philomel Books,
an imprint of Penguin Random House LLC, 2021

Copyright © 2021 by T. A. Barron

Map copyright © 2000 by Ian Schoenherr

Penguin supports copyright. Copyright fuels creativity, encourages diverse voices, promotes free speech, and
creates a vibrant culture. Thank you for buying an authorized edition of this book and for complying with
copyright laws by not reproducing, scanning, or distributing any part of it in any form without permission. You
are supporting writers and allowing Penguin to continue to publish books for every reader.

Philomel Books is a registered trademark of Penguin Random House LLC.

Visit us online at penguinrandomhouse.com.

Library of Congress Cataloging-in-Publication Data is available.

Printed in Canada

ISBN 9780593203491

10 9 8 7 6 5 4 3 2 1

FRI

Edited by Kelsey Murphy

Design by Monique Sterling

Text set in MarcoPolo

This book is a work of fiction. Any references to historical events, real people, or real places are used fictitiously.
Other names, characters, places, and events are products of the author's imagination, and any resemblance to
actual events or places or persons, living or dead, is entirely coincidental.

The publisher does not have any control over and does not assume any responsibility for author or third-party
websites or their content.

To
all the little giants
I've known and loved

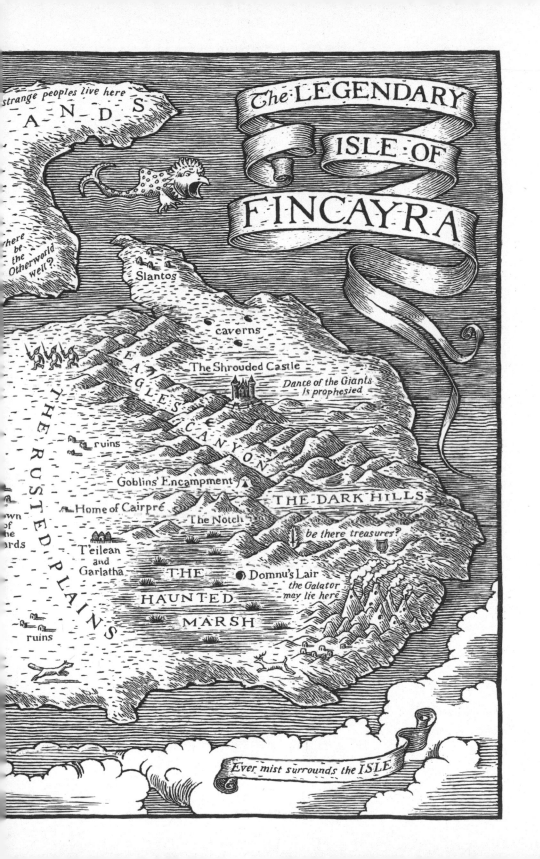

The LEGENDARY
ISLE OF
FINCAYRA

strange peoples live here

A N D S

where be the Otherworld well?

Slantos

caverns

The Shrouded Castle

Dance of the Giants is prophesied

E A G L E S   C A N Y O N

ruins

Goblins' Encampment

THE DARK HILLS

Home of Cairpré

The Notch

be there treasures?

T'eilean and Garlatha

THE

Domnu's Lair

the Galator may lie here

HAUNTED

MARSH

T H E   R U S T E D   P L A I N S

wn of he rds

ruins

Ever mist surrounds the ISLE

CONTENTS

A SPECIAL MESSAGE...

Shim is my name—and a grandly name it is, deserving all the praise it never got. Certainly, definitely, absolutely!

But my original name was muchly bigger. Just as my original self was muchly bigger—a long way from the smallsy, utterly shrunkelled self who first met Merlin. How did that change really happen?

That is the story I'd like to tell you now. It's the tale of a verily small person . . . with some verily big dreams.

I.

BIG FEET

"Seventeen boulders!" crowed the midwife Gargolyn. Though she herself was a giant, she strained to lift the squirming baby in her hands. "That's a hefty weight for a newlyborn, even for a giant."

Turning slowly in the sunlight, Gargolyn observed the baby closely, from his pudgy nose down to his unusually large feet. True to the giants' ancient traditions, the baby's mother, Vonya, had chosen to give birth outdoors. It had been a long pregnancy, lasting thirteen months—but here they were at last, in the roofless, open-air Birthing Pavilion.

Set in the middle of a garden and walled by hedges, the Pavilion was encircled by columns that had been carved centuries before from a hillside of silver quartz, the sparkling white rock that Fincayrans called giant-stone. Those majestic columns reached skyward to the height of medium-size spruce trees—which is to say they reached only up to the elbows of most fully grown giants. On each column were carvings of paired faces— one belonging to a famous giant, about whom bards had sung songs and told stories for ages, and the other belonging to that giant's mother . . . who had, in most cases, given birth right here at this very place.

"Hefty weight indeed," Vonya declared, a proud smile on her face. Carefully, she raised her enormous bulk higher on the mattress stuffed with willow boughs and rushes. "Now give him back to his mother, you hear? Before you drop that weight on your toes."

Wrinkling her leathery brow, the midwife scowled. Even as she trembled with the weight, she grumbled, "I've held hundreds of babies in my time, and never dropped a single one."

Vonya reached her arms, as thick and sturdy as tree trunks, toward her baby. "I'm sure that's true . . . but not many of them weighed as much as half a mountain."

"Right." Gargolyn's scowl melted into a grin. "In fact, none of them was as big at birth as this one." As she passed the baby over to Vonya, she added, "Half his weight, I daresay, is from these plumpish feet. Just look at the size of them!"

As if on cue, the baby kicked wildly, almost smacking the midwife's nose.

"At least half." Vonya chuckled as she took the baby and folded her strong arms around him. "I'm tempted to call him Big Feet . . . until he earns his true name."

"No, too irreverent," said the old midwife, shaking her ropes of gray hair. "A young giant deserves a nick-name that's more, well, *respectable*. Something befitting a member of Fincayra's oldest race—the island's first people, the ones our great spirit Dagda carved out of the holy mountain."

"I know, I know," Vonya replied. "But sometimes the old traditions need a new look. Even our creation stories need to be rewritten from time to time."

"Nonsense," Gargolyn sputtered. "What kind of mother would teach her child such silliness?"

"This one," declared Vonya. Brushing back her auburn

curls, which looked more like a wild bramble bush than a head of hair, she peered closely at her child. His pink eyes stared up at her, bright with life and curiosity . . . and also a hint of mischief.

"Well, hello, my little jelly roll," she cooed. "Something tells me you're going to be writing a whole lot of new stories with your life."

The baby giant blinked his eyes, slowly and meaningfully, almost as if he understood.

Vonya sighed, slumping a bit on the willow mattress. "I only wish your papa could be here to see you." She wiped her huge forearm across her eyes. "He'd have loved to play with your chubby toes."

Like a tall tree that suddenly folded itself down to a smaller size, Gargolyn knelt beside the young mother and her baby. Although her old knees cracked so loud they frightened a nearby family of rabbits, who scampered away to hide in the hedges, the midwife spoke softly and gently. "My dear, I feel your loss. Jonkl was a great giant—and he would have made a very fine papa."

Vonya drew a halting breath. "He told me to be brave . . . that day when he left to fight against Gawr." She wiped her eyes again. "He just didn't say how brave."

Gargolyn's wrinkled hand touched her shoulder. "When our wizardking Tuatha asked us to send our strongest giants to help him defeat the evil warlord Gawr, we all knew there was great risk. And when your Jonkl left, he knew he was fighting for all of us . . . including your child."

"I just wish . . ." said Vonya in a whisper that seemed impossibly soft for a fully grown giant, "that I could see him again . . . and show him our son."

"Someday you will," assured the older giant. "In the Realm of the Spirits. Without doubt, he is there right now, standing next to Dagda. And," she added with a nod at the varied faces carved into the columns, "with the spirits of all these great giants who came before."

She paused, looking at Vonya with compassion. "He knows, I'm sure, that his great bravery helped Tuatha win that battle and drive away Gawr."

With her free hand, Gargolyn gestured toward the immense stone towers and buildings, fountains and gates, visible beyond the Pavilion. "Thanks to him, we are safe here in Varigal. All of us . . . including his beloved wife and child."

Vonya nodded slowly, then turned back to the baby

in her arms. Looking deep into his eyes, she said, "Now we must be brave together, you and I."

Even as he gazed up at her, the baby giant reached out his hand and wrapped it tightly around his mother's thumb. Astonished, she caught her breath. Was that just a coincidence? Or had that tiny little hand just made a gesture with giant-size meaning?

"I daresay," she told her son, "you will give us some very special stories."

2.

TWELVE YEARS LATER

"Hold still now, Big Feet!"

Vonya struggled not to impale her son with her sewing needle, made from the rib of a whale whose body had washed ashore last winter on Fincayra's southern coast, as she tried valiantly to mend his torn britches. That job was difficult enough because he was still wearing them—and even more difficult because of his enormous size. Though just twelve years old, Big Feet already stood taller than all the other young giants in Varigal, and half a human height taller than the imposing lass whose nickname was Sister Behemoth. Even now, bent over so his mother could work on the ripped barkcloth covering his backside, his rump rose up like a miniature mountain.

"Why won't you take these off so I can mend them properly?" Vonya pleaded.

"Because if I took them off, I'd surely and purely rip them again."

"This is the third time this week I've had to stitch you up," she grumbled, pulling on her vine thread.

"And probobily not the last one, neither," he declared in his unique vernacular. "I'm muchly good at throwing and stomping and other giantly things . . . but I'm *especially* good at ripping my britches!"

Though completely bent over, with his forehead resting on the grassy turf, his whole body quaked as he chuckled at his joke.

"Quit laughing, will you?" Vonya shook her head so hard that her earrings, consisting of three wagon wheels hanging from each ear, knocked loudly, like tree branches smacking together in a storm. "I need you to stay still."

But he kept on chuckling mirthfully.

"If you don't stop, I'm going to stab you with this needle."

"That would hurtly something awful," he replied, finally seeing the wisdom in her words. For good measure, he added, "Certainly, definitely, absolutely!"

A few minutes later, she finished, tying off the vine thread. Giving a smack to his rump, she declared, "All right now. Try to keep these britches intact for at least another day or two."

The lad stood up, rising to his full gargantuan height. Though still a young adult, he stood just as tall as his parent. He grinned at her, crinkling his nose, as he decided to give her a special nickname. "I will, my one and only Motherly."

Unable to suppress her own grin, she nodded. "Motherly, is it? Well, that's just as unique as everything else you say. You can call me that . . . so long as I can still call you my jelly roll."

He rolled his eyes. "I'm way too bigly for that now! Can't you call me something more grownupish? More, you know, *maturely*?"

"No," she said flatly. "Now you go and find yourself some fun. Any ideas?"

He glanced over his shoulder at the mountainous terrain beyond the towering stone buildings. "Well, I'll just go find something giantly to do. Maybe I'll throw some boulders at the moon? Or shout thunderly across a canyon to scare some wyverns?"

Vonya shook her head, clinking her wagon wheel earrings again. "Stay away from any wyverns, you hear? They may be smaller than most dragons, but a pack of them can maim or kill a giant—even one as big as you."

He scowled. "No wyverns could everly hurt me. I'm so bigly, more bigly by the day! And someday . . . I'll be the bigliest giant in history, higher than the highliest tree."

With a sigh, she looked at him lovingly. "Probably true. But it won't happen if you get mauled by wyverns. Do you understand?"

"No." Squaring his shoulders, he twisted a bare foot into the ground, crushing several rocks under his weight. "You still treat me like a child—always so worriedly."

"That's because you *are* my child." She looked at him soulfully. "My only child."

"But I'm not a baby!"

"That's for sure," she said with the hint of a grin. "No baby could hold so much food as you do. Especially—"

"Honey!" The thought of his most favorite thing to

eat suddenly perked him up. "Methinks I'll go find a munchily log full of honey."

"Good idea. Off you go now! Just mind your britches, all right?"

"Certainly, definitely, absolutely!"

He turned and strode off, his thoughts already dripping with honeyed anticipation. In less than a minute, he thumped down Varigal's central street and through the market square, a place that always hummed with activity. On some days, like today, it held merchants' carts from all across the island; on other occasions, it hosted the giants' public meetings and boisterous celebrations.

Seconds later, Big Feet passed through the city's main gates. He nodded in greeting to the pair of guards, and they tipped their tall treespears in return. Striding past them, he left the walled city and entered the wild lands beyond.

With a bounce in his step, he headed toward the nearest hill. Pursing his lips, he thought about the conversation he'd just had with his mother. She didn't understand how much he'd grown—not just in size, but in maturity. Why, he was almost an adult! What he needed now was not protection but freedom. Independence. And something else, something that called to him more every day.

"Adventure," he declared as he strode up the slope. "That's what I'd like, muchly more than anything."

Reaching the crest of the hill, he raised his bulbous nose and sniffed the air. Like most giants, he was blessed with an extraordinary sense of smell . . . and this spot offered a rich array of aromas.

The first smells that came to him were from trees— the sweet sap of spruce, the calming scent of beech, the pungent odor of harshflower. Then . . . an owl's nest, in the hollow of a tree somewhere nearby, full of crumpled feathers, mouse bones, moist moss, and old eggshells. A family of porcupines out foraging, their quills sticky with sap. The remains of a lightning strike, over on the next hill perhaps, smelling like charred wood and burned grass. A foxes' den, crammed with meat scraps and sinew from last night's meal.

Suddenly, his nose quivered. An electric thrill passed through him, exciting his whole body.

Honey! he realized. Not far away from here . . . maybe on the other side of that rocky ravine.

He strode across the top of the hill, covering the distance in just a few steps of his massive feet. Down the slope he crashed, flattening bushes and windblown branches under his weight. Following the sweet scent, he hopped across the ravine, pausing only to kick a boulder that sat precariously on the edge. It smashed on the opposite side, frightening a herd of deer grazing in the shadows below. Instantly, they bolted off down the ravine.

The young giant veered to the right, plunged through a grove of pines—and stopped abruptly at the edge of a marsh. He smacked his lips with satisfaction . . . as well as anticipation.

There, right in front of him, stood the broken trunk of an old sycamore. Hundreds of bees hovered around the trunk, buzzing loudly. For a few seconds, he stood there, taller than the remains of the tree, a hungry gleam in his eyes.

"Time for hollowings and swallowings," he declared. Stepping up to the honey tree, he plunged his hand down into the broken top. Shards of wood and bark exploded in all directions, while honey oozed from every knothole. The bees, meanwhile, panicked and buzzed excitedly, swarming around the gargantuan creature who had dared to attack their hive.

Big Feet, however, didn't mind. "Noisy little buzzers! Don't you know my skin is way too thick to get stingded?" For an instant, he wondered how much more vulnerable to bee stings someone smaller would be. "But I is bigly, much too bigly to care!"

He pulled his hand out of the tree, which made a loud slurping noise. Honey, gooey and golden, pooled in his palm and slid down his fingers. Eagerly, he swallowed the sweet substance. Then he licked his fingers clean and, disregarding the enraged bees, plunged his hand back into the tree. After several more swallows, he grinned happily, his chin dripping with rivers of honey . . . and his craving at least temporarily satisfied.

Turning to go, he waved to the bees. "Don't be so angrily, little buzzers. I left you plenty." His grin widened as he thought, *That is, until I come back again.*

Just then he heard a familiar sound. Voices—giants' voices—called excitedly from somewhere in the distance. With a last lick of his fingers, he strode off to find the source. For those voices had the distinct ring of adventure.

3.

THE LIVING MIST

Following the voices, Big Feet hurried toward the huge precipice called Giants' Cliffs that marked the western coast of Fincayra. His thunderous footsteps shook loose several boulders, sending them crashing down into ravines. A flock of crows, frightened by him passing by their rowan tree, took off in an eruption of black wings and cacophonous caws.

As he walked, he noticed his shadow moving along with him, changing its size constantly with the terrain and angle of the sun. At times, it stretched out immensely, growing bigger than any tree. And at other times, it shrank down to almost nothing—just a dark patch underfoot.

What sort of giant will I be? he wondered. Not just in his body . . . but in his heart. Would he be enormous in both ways, like the father he never knew? Would he ever do something important enough to earn a true name, one that would have made his father proud?

He swallowed, trying to get rid of the strange lump in his throat. Or would he turn out to be just a big, hulking person whose mind wasn't bright and whose heart wasn't true?

Just then he saw the unmistakable shapes of three more giants. They stood near the edge of the cliffs, silhouetted against the wall of mist that surrounded Fincayra's coast. Like all Fincayrans, Big Feet knew that the mist made an impenetrable barrier around the isle, hiding it from view of any foolish mortals who might try to sail across the ocean in search of this legendary island where magic still reigned supreme.

More importantly, he knew that this mist was itself alive with magic—and that the Living Mist held powers not even the wizardking Tuatha could fully comprehend. Some believed the mist's mind was exclusively bent on protecting the isle from any intruders, especially those who might want to use it as a bridge to cross from the Earth into the Spirit Realm. Others, including his mother, believed that the Living Mist could also predict the future . . . and did so in surprising ways.

"You there!" he boomed as he approached the others. "Are you gaming?"

"Yes indeed," called one, waving enthusiastically. "Come join us!"

Big Feet recognized Greeno immediately. That wasn't hard, since this particular young giant made up for his lack of height by sheer girth and a green mane that fell over his shoulders, which made him look like a huge boulder topped by flowing moss.

The other two giants spun around as their friend approached. While nearly the same age as Big Feet and Greeno, they gave the appearance of being older. Lumpster's arms bulged with muscles—and while he didn't use his brain all that much, he frequently used those arms to break rocks, shake trees, and toss unlucky cows into the air. And Sister Behemoth, second only to Big Feet in height among the young giants, always carried herself with the air of an adult . . . until she opened her mouth to speak.

"Looky, looky," she called in her thin, squeaky voice. "Watch me throw this rock through there!"

Hefting a stone in her massive hand, she turned toward a dark hole in the wall of mist. Like a vaporous target, the hole contracted and expanded . . . as if the Living Mist was teasing her to try to score a bull's-eye.

"Give your best shot," called Lumpster, trying to crack open a rock by hitting it against his head.

"But beware of that edge," added Greeno. "You're standing pretty close."

Shaking her massive head in defiance, Sister Behemoth cried shrilly, "Don't tell me what to do!" She moved even closer to the cliff edge, which plunged straight down for the height of twenty giants to the crashing surf below.

Big Feet joined them, striding up gleefully. Immediately, he noticed a crack forming in the ledge right beneath her feet. "Sister!" he shouted. "Be carefully!"

She ignored him, concentrating her aim at the misty hole. Just as she raised her arm to throw—

The ledge broke off! Rocks crumbled under her enormous weight, plunging down to the surf. The young giant shrieked wildly, flailing her arms as she started to fall.

Slam! Big Feet grabbed her forearm, clasping tight. He held on to her with all his strength. But quickly her weight started to drag him over the edge. Madly, he dug his free hand and his toes into the ground, but still she pulled him closer and closer to the cliff edge.

"Grab me!" he called urgently to the others. "Before she drags me over!"

Lumpster and Greeno, who'd been standing frozen in shock, suddenly revived. They leaped on Big Feet, grabbing his arm and leg. Together they tugged, grunting and moaning. Lumpster's muscles flexed so much he popped every button on his barkcloth shirt, while Greeno's hair turned brown from rubbing in the dirt.

Slowly, bit by bit, they hauled their friends back. Meanwhile, Big Feet held on tight to Sister's forearm, although his hand hurt so much it seemed to scream. Making his job harder, she couldn't stop wriggling and twisting as she tried to climb back up to the top.

"Stop your squigwiggling," he groaned. "You're making this worse!"

But taking advice wasn't something Sister ever liked to do—and she wasn't going to start now. She twisted more violently than ever. Big Feet's grip loosened . . . and his hand felt ready to explode.

Finally, when he thought he couldn't hang on for another second, Sister's forehead lifted above the cliff edge. Then came her face, her shoulders, and finally—with a last big tug—her chest and legs. Still squirming wildly, she rolled over on the ground next to Big Feet. Together with their exhausted companions, they lay on their backs, panting hard.

Several seconds passed before Big Feet felt strong enough to sit up. When he did, he found himself face-to-face with Sister, who was watching him with an unmistakable look of gratitude.

"You caught me," she said, her voice even more squeaky than usual. "I would have surely . . ."

"Died," he finished. "Certainly and for sure. You'd have been utterly smush-killed."

Embarrassed, she glanced over at the wall of mist—and the dark hole she'd been so determined to hit. "Thanks to you, I can still breathe . . . and run . . . and dance. And also do this."

She leaned over and planted a big, wet kiss on his cheek.

Surprised, he drew back, not really sure he'd liked

that experience. And yet . . . even as he wiped the dripping saliva off his cheek, his pink eyes shone a bit brighter.

Lumpster sat up right then, just in time to see the kiss. Excitedly, he asked, "What about me? I helped, too." He puckered his lips.

"Eeewww," squealed Sister. "No way!"

With a sigh, Lumpster grunted. "Didn't really want it, anyway."

"Want what?" asked Greeno, who had finally recovered enough to sit up. He shook his head, scattering pebbles everywhere and releasing a cloud of dirt.

"Nothing," said Sister. She gave Big Feet a sly wink. "Nothing at all."

Maybe it was the thrill of saving his friend's life . . . or the surprise of getting his first kiss. Whatever the reason, Big Feet felt excited. Validated, like he was someone worthy. Like he could stand even a bit taller.

Rising to his feet, he spontaneously picked up a rock. He took only a brief glance at the mist, then reared back and threw the rock as far as he could. It whizzed through the air—and passed straight through the hole in the mist. Bull's-eye!

"By Dagda's beard," said Sister, totally astonished. "Amazing shot!"

"Yeah," agreed Lumpster. "That's by far the best thing you've done today."

Sister shot him a murderous glance. Fortunately, Lumpster didn't see it. (And quite possibly, he wouldn't have understood what she meant even if he had.)

Big Feet merely nodded in satisfaction. This day had indeed turned out just fine. Maybe better than just fine. He drew a deep, contented breath.

Gazing out at the wall of Living Mist, he watched its shifting contours. The hole melted away, swiftly disappearing in the vapors. Then he noticed something strange: Where the hole had been, a misty face appeared—one with wild hair and a large, potato-like nose. His own face!

He gasped in surprise. The face looked right at him, encircled by clouds of vapor, watching him so intently it seemed to read his very thoughts. Its mouth, so much like his own, grinned with satisfaction.

All at once, everything changed. The grin suddenly shifted, turning into a scowl—and then a wide-open mouth that seemed to scream in anguish. The mouth contorted, twisting unnaturally.

This looked so real to Big Feet that he felt a sharp bolt of pain slice through his entire body. In that instant, he felt nothing else—only the pain.

He shuddered, reeling, barely able to stand. Yet he kept his eyes fixed on the misty face. What he saw next, though, hurt even more.

The face started to shrink down in size, growing smaller and smaller by the second. All the while, the misty mouth seemed to scream in agony. Finally, when the face had shrunken down to the size of a tiny dot—it vanished completely, swallowed by the swirling mist.

Shaken to his core, Big Feet collapsed. He sat on the ground, peering dazedly at the Living Mist, wondering what he'd just seen.

Turning to Sister, he asked weakly, "Did you see that?"

"Sure, I did. You threw a stone right through that hole!"

Blinking, he turned to the others. But their expressions, like Sister's, showed only jubilation. How could that be? Could he somehow have just imagined that face, that scream, that brutal experience of shrinking down to nothing?

Sister clapped him playfully on the shoulder. "Come on, let's go back to Varigal."

"Yeah," chimed in Greeno. "I'm ready for supper."

At that, Lumpster smacked his lips hungrily.

"You all go ahead," Big Feet said weakly, with as much casualness as he could muster. "I want to stay here a littlish while . . . by myself."

4.

ELF

The trio of young giants stomped off together, leaving Big Feet seated at the edge of the cliff that dropped straight down to the sea. Neither Lumpster nor Greeno looked back, as their thoughts had turned entirely to supper. Only Sister paused, glancing over her shoulder at their forlorn companion who now sat alone, gazing at the swirling mist.

She almost called to him. But sensing he needed some space, she caught herself. With a grunt, she turned and hurried to rejoin the others. Their footsteps shook the ground like minor earthquakes, slowly fading as they departed.

Meanwhile, Big Feet peered at the shifting vapors beyond the cliff. The Living Mist billowed and contorted, making endless shapes that only its mysterious mind could understand.

Did I really see that face? the young giant wondered. *That screaming, shrinking face?*

But of course, he knew what he'd seen. Just as surely as he sensed that right now, out there, the Living Mist was laughing at him. The air almost crackled with mirth.

He shuddered, feeling another bolt of pain in his chest. How could someone as huge as himself ever shrink down to nothingness? It wasn't possible! Not in a million years!

Yet he hadn't imagined that brutal experience. And he could smell, mixed in with all the scents of the sea far below, a whiff of fear.

Shaken, he rose to his feet. With a grimace, he turned his back on the Living Mist and started to plod away. Behind him, the swirling vapors darkened to a thick, leaden gray.

Aimlessly, he wandered back into the forest. With his thoughts still on that frightful visage in the mist, he paid no attention to where he was going. It didn't even occur to him that he was heading away from Varigal, where his mother—as well as his supper—waited for him.

He kept plodding, absently following the contours of a steep ravine. His bare feet crushed branches and kicked aside fallen trunks. Around him, the trees seemed to sigh knowingly. No longer did he watch his shadow on the ground, sensing instead a shadow inside, one that darkened his thoughts.

"Am I actually a bigly person?" he wondered aloud. "Or really just a smallsy person in a bigly body?"

He continued to trudge along. A herd of Fincayran blue-antlered elk scattered to get out of his way. A yellow snake, annoyed at having to uncoil and leave a comfortable rock, hissed and slid into a nearby hole. An immense owl, holding a freshly caught mouse in her beak, took flight and glided silently over to her nest in the hollow of a cypress tree.

Suddenly—a piercing shriek cut through the forest. He halted in his tracks, instantly recognizing the shrill, angry cry made by only one kind of beast.

A wyvern!

He ran toward the sound, scaling the ravine and

topping the next rise in just a few giant-size bounds. As the shrieking grew louder, he started to hear other, very different sounds, as well—thunderous booms and crashes, along with a chorus of tiny voices that cried out in agony.

Bursting out of the trees into a clearing, he saw the wyvern—a powerful one with gleaming purple scales that covered his entire body from the tips of his jagged wings to the heavy ball of bone at the end of his tail. Shrieking wildly, the purple wyvern lunged repeatedly at a deep cavern in an immense outcropping of giantstone. As his wings slapped the air, his deadly claws slashed at the cavern entrance, breaking off chunks of stone.

Small, winged creatures, glowing bright blue but moving too fast for Big Feet to see clearly, buzzed around the wyvern's head. All the while, the little beings wailed piteously. Sometimes the wyvern's jaws snapped closed on them, abruptly ending their lives. More of them fell from his slapping wings. With every passing second, their numbers lessened, their glow forever extinguished.

The wyvern kept slashing at the cavern, clearly searching for something. Suddenly, he reared back and slammed the ball of his tail against the entrance, smashing the outcropping so hard that several boulders broke off, crushing more of the glowing blue creatures. All the while, the dragon-like beast screeched furiously—a cry meant to freeze anyone nearby in terror.

But not Big Feet. Enraged by this brutality, he roared and ran headlong into battle. He threw all his weight into the charge, slamming full force into the wyvern's shoulder.

Shrieking louder than ever, the surprised beast rolled backward, slicing his jaw on a sharp edge of stone. Purple blood oozed from the wound. The wyvern whirled around to face his attacker, blood dripping from his lower lip, fires of revenge burning in his eyes.

Big Feet, who had been thrown backward by the impact, rolled aside—just in time to avoid the wyvern's tail, which smashed down on that very spot. Leaping up, he grabbed a huge boulder and hurled it at the wyvern. The beast jumped, but the boulder clipped one wing, ripping off a whole row of scales that sprinkled the ground amidst bits of stone and the bodies of lifeless little beings.

Raging, the wyvern whipped his jagged wings and brandished his claws, preparing to attack. All his thoughts were now bent on just one goal: revenge.

Remembering Vonya's warning, Big Feet knew that a single slice from those claws could sever his arm—or worse. He lunged for another boulder, even bigger than the first. With all his strength, he lifted it to throw. But this rock was so heavy that he wobbled unsteadily. Then he lost his balance, tumbling over on the ground.

The wyvern snarled, sensing victory. Knowing that his enemy would soon perish, the beast's eyes flamed brighter. Slowly, he raised his claws, poised to vanquish this bold young giant who had dared to intrude.

Just as the wyvern was about to leap—he noticed a small, shiny object at the edge of the cavern. Shimmering with a strange, orange glow, this object caught his full attention. A greedy rumble reverberated in the wyvern's throat as he stared, spellbound.

Taking advantage of the delay, Big Feet stood up. He braced himself and grasped the boulder again, lifting it high enough to throw. With every fiber of his muscles, he hurled it at the wyvern.

In a flash, the wyvern dodged the boulder and leaped—not at Big Feet, but at the orange prize that had caught his attention. Grasping the object in his claws, he took off with a last, triumphant shriek that shook the nearby trees. As he flew away, blood still dripping from his jaw, he cast a vengeful glance back at the unexpected foe who had caused so much trouble.

Big Feet stared back at the departing wyvern. Though shaky from all the stress of battle, he stood as tall as possible. And tall was what he felt again—no longer the small, screaming likeness that he'd seen in the mist, but a giant in every way. Big enough—and brave enough—to scare off a wyvern!

Then, looking down, he caught his breath. That terrible bully had destroyed dozens of innocent lives. Tiny, broken bodies lay scattered everywhere. Some still had their delicate blue wings attached, while others were torn to shreds. None of them showed any signs of life.

Faeries! Recognizing them from the stories Vonya had told him, he bent down to look closer. Though their only movement now came from the gentle breeze that stirred their broken and tattered wings, he knew that these tiny blue beings had once been among the most beautiful and graceful creatures in all of Fincayra.

Luminous faeries, he said to himself, recalling their species name. Like all the other kinds of faeries, wondrous beings who lived in watery places or moss carpets or starflower meadows across the island, these faeries had translucent wings and elegant antennae . . . and their own special magic. But no other kind had magic to equal that of the luminous faeries. For these faeries could actually produce their own light—glowing as they flew, like small, winged stars.

A tiny flicker of blue light over by the cavern caught his eye. Barely perceptible, it seemed no more than a single spark, probably just the light glinting on a shard of stone. Nevertheless, he moved closer to investigate.

He gasped. It came from a faery! Though bedraggled and smudged with dirt, the tiny creature flickered ever so slightly. Pale blue light glowed on her whole body, from the tip of her nose to the edges of her wings, which seemed as evanescent as rainbows.

With greatest care, Big Feet picked up the faery and held her in the palm of his hand. Smaller than his thumbnail, she quivered, glowing weakly. Slowly, she seemed to revive, straightening her two antennae, which each ended with a rounded knob that resembled a bell. Gold in color, those bell-shaped knobs were the only parts of her that weren't radiant blue.

The faery's light grew stronger, bit by bit. Finally,

she opened her eyes, which shone as bright blue as the sunlit sky.

For several heartbeats, the faery looked up at Big Feet. Then she shook her antennae—and a slow, somber ringing filled the air. For those golden knobs were indeed bells. And now they rang out in sorrow.

"My family," moaned the little faery, in a voice so quiet it was barely a whisper. "My family—my whole colony—attacked without any warning! By that . . . that . . ."

"Wyvern," finished the giant. "They is truly bad, horribobilous things."

Leaning his face closer, so that his bulbous nose almost touched the delicate creature in his hand, he said softly, "I'm so verily sorry for you."

The faery ceased ringing her antennae bells. Peering up at the giant, she said sadly, "Today I lost everything. My family, my home . . . everything."

She paused, quivering. "But I also found something."

"What?"

"Someone very brave."

Big Feet blushed, his nose turning bright red. "You is muchly too kind. All I did was—"

"Try. You tried to help." Looking deep into his eyes, she added, "Thank you."

"You're welcome, little friend. Certainly, definitely, absolutely."

Her strength regained, she beat her glowing wings and floated gracefully upward. She glanced at the terrible destruction around them, her wings whirring so fast they looked like a pair of tiny blue clouds upon her back. Once again, her bells chimed sorrowfully.

After a moment, she turned back to him and said softly, "I'm glad to have met you, big friend."

He nodded. "Me too, ever so muchly."

The sound of her golden bells lightened a bit, almost to a ring of gratitude. "Go now . . . and live with light."

"You too, little flier." Scrunching his nose in thought, he said, "Little friend, little flier . . . could I maybily just call you LF?"

"Elf? That's a pretty strange name for a faery. But sure, if that's what you'd like." She floated closer, hovering above his nose. "And what shall I call you?"

"Big Friend is good enough. Certainly, definitely, absolutely."

5.

BRIGHT FLAMES

Dusk was deepening by the time Big Feet approached the city gates, covering the surrounding hills with veils of shadow. Even before he left the forest's mesh of trees, he saw the bright flames of the bonfire. Reaching high above the walls of giantstone that surrounded Varigal, the flames slapped at the darkening sky and shot sparks upward.

Young though he was, he'd seen a few such bonfires before. And he knew that those flames rising from the city's vast market square could mean only one thing.

Celebration! he thought gleefully. Something special must be happening tonight.

Then he realized, with a tingle of delight, that every celebration meant *food*. Lots and lots of tasty, mouthwatering food.

Indeed, as he strode through the main gates, he caught the scent of roasting ubermushrooms . . . one of his most favorite treats. Fincayra's largest mushrooms, they grew only in the darkest groves of spruce and swelled to the size of a giant's fist. Roasted on an open fire, glazed with thick apple cider, and dusted with tarragon and thyme, they had always delighted him. Especially when he dipped them in honey . . . which he did with almost every kind of food.

As he turned into the market square, the enormous bonfire crackled and snapped ferociously—reminding him, for an instant, of the wyvern's angry snarls. But that memory quickly vanished, replaced by all the colorful sights and wondrous smells of a festive celebration.

Giants of every description filled the square, some of them standing taller than the stone columns holding intricate sculptures, carved by skilled giants long gone. Wearing colorful hats and vests and capes made from rough barkcloth or silken grasses, they traded stories and jokes around the bonfire, jostled each other in games, swilled barrel-size flasks of ale, or hurled fallen trees onto the flames. One pair of giants, twin sisters with lavender hair and square jaws, made soulful music with their enormous fiddles, while giants young and old danced to the songs. The two guards from the gates arrived, having left their posts to join the fun; immediately, they set aside their treespears and picked up huge flasks of foamy ale.

Over by the gargantuan tables loaded with food, Sister Behemoth waved enthusiastically at Big Feet. He waved back, somewhat awkwardly, not wanting to tempt her to give him another kiss. Then he spied Lumpster and Greeno, who were busy throwing sacks of grain at a painting of a wide-eyed dragon on the side of a building. One sack burst open and sprayed grain all over a surprised old fellow who was juggling several of the biggest garlics Big Feet had ever seen.

Continuing to maneuver through the crowd, he nearly tripped over a giant who was lying on her back while someone painted her face with radiant colors. At last, he spotted the person he most wanted to see.

"Motherly!" he called, seeing Vonya in animated conversation with her good friend Umdahla, whose azure-blue hair was unmistakable.

Vonya promptly said goodbye to Umdahla and strode over to join him. Clearly dressed for the occasion, she had tied back her bushy hair with a rope and decorated it with white pelican feathers. She wore a handsome plaid blouse and her finest barkcloth skirt. And in the spirit of celebration, she had donned her favorite wagon wheels, all painted bright yellow, three on each ear.

"My son," she said as she hugged him to her chest. "Back from your outing, are you?"

"Yes indeedily."

She studied him with care. "You look different. Maybe," she added with a twinkle, "you're feeling even more grown-up?"

He almost grinned. "Mostly I'm feeling hungrily!"

"Go eat, then." Vonya nodded, clinking her wagon wheel earrings. "You've earned your supper."

As he started to walk toward the food tables, he paused and asked, "What's this celebration about, anyway?"

She merely chuckled. "Go eat. I'll tell you later."

Needing no more encouragement, he jogged over

to the ubermushrooms turning on a spit by the bon-fire. Even as he approached, the giant who was roasting them—a wide-shouldered fellow whose nickname, Sideways, came from how he needed to turn to pass through any doorway—greeted him merrily.

"Come fer some tasty mushers, have ye, laddie?"

Big Feet nodded enthusiastically. With a practiced twist, Sideways speared a freshly roasted mushroom and tossed it over. The young giant smiled gratefully as he caught it, then immediately dunked it in a huge tub of honey.

Seconds later, he bit into the treat and savored its sweetness as honey dribbled down his chin. He made quick work of the mushroom—and then did the same to two more.

Moving to the food tables, he drained a wooden flask of pear cider before gobbling down a plate of lemon-leaf wraps filled with minced elk. Barely pausing to take a breath, he downed a cinnamon doughnut as big as his nose, a bowl of cashew meganuts, two slices of still-steaming apple pie (sweetened with extra honey, of course), a gigantic slab of mountain goat cheese, one overflowing handful of fried locusts (commonly called "crunchybugs"), and half of an enormous sea trout stuffed with hot chili peppers. Plus, for good measure, another honey-dipped mushroom.

He licked his sticky fingers—more to catch every last drop of honey than to clean them. Just then, above the din, he heard a familiar voice.

"Big Feet!" called Vonya. "Come over here."

Still licking his fingers, he sallied to her side. "I never get tired of hearing you call my name."

She peered at him, a mysterious glint in her eyes. "Ah, but that's the last time I will ever call you Big Feet."

Confused, he sputtered, "What? Why everly . . . what? Why?"

Vonya drew a deep breath and said proudly, "This big celebration is because someone earned his true name today."

"Really? Who?"

She ruffled his scraggly mane. "*You*, my dear. This celebration is for you!"

"Me?" he asked, still confused.

"Yes indeed. Word has it you saved somebody's life today."

He blinked at her in amazement. "How could you

everly know that? And besides," he added modestly, "she was really tiny—very, very smallsy."

"Small?" she retorted, her turn to be confused. "Are you kidding?"

"No. After all, she fit snuggishly in my hand. Wings included!"

"What in the world do you mean? We're talking about Sister Behemoth! You saved her life at the cliffs, didn't you?

"Oh, that! Yes, I did." He beamed, finally understanding. "Forgive me, Motherly. I've had a busily day saving people."

"Evidently." Her smile then melted away. "But there's one thing I just can't forgive you for."

He hunched defensively. "What terribibulous thing did I do this time?"

She tried to look at him sternly . . . but that only lasted an instant. "You ripped your britches again!"

Pulling him close, she tousled his hair and said softly, "I don't care a bit, my jelly roll. And I'm very, very proud of you."

He relaxed into her hug. For the first time this busy day, he felt neither very big nor very small. All he felt right now was . . . loved.

"After what you've done today," she said gently, "I believe you've learned the most important thing about being a giant."

"What's that?"

Just then someone tossed another tree on the bonfire, making the flames rise even higher than before. Her face aglow in the reflection, she answered with a single sentence: "Bigness means more than the size of your bones."

6.

TRUE NAME

Big Feet pulled himself back from Vonya's embrace. Pondering her face, so bright in the bonfire's flames, he asked, "Bigness isn't about your bones? What in the worldly world does *that* mean?"

Before she could reply, someone shouted—loud enough for even a gathering of festive giants to hear. "Attention, all of you! Attention!"

Heads turned in the speaker's direction. Conversations stopped midsentence; those eating fish and doughnuts and mushrooms paused; even wrestling adolescents froze. Lumpster, who was just about to throw another bag of grain at the wall, turned abruptly—too abruptly, as it happened, since he hurled the bag right at the juggler, flattening him and sending all his garlics flying.

"Thank you," declared the speaker, who was standing on top of a wooden platform used by merchants in the market square.

A rough-looking fellow with tree branches braided into his hair and a belly the size of a boulder, he seemed entirely comfortable being the center of attention. Though he'd long ago earned his true name, everyone called him Blaster for his extraordinarily loud voice. Because of that quality, in fact, he'd been elected the mayor of Varigal. For what could possibly be more important than a loud voice to call to order a meeting of rowdy giants?

"We are gathered tonight for a very special occasion!" So loud did he bellow that hundreds of pigeons, roosting in the rafters of the nearby buildings, took off in a frightened whir of wings.

"And that is," Blaster continued, "to give someone his true name. One of the youngest giants in history ever to gain such an honor."

Raising his hand, he pointed. "I mean you, Big Feet.

We've all heard about your bravery today at the cliffs."

"It's true!" shouted Sister Behemoth in her squeaky voice. "He saved my life!"

Blushing so much that his nose could have been mistaken for a ripe sweet potato, Big Feet shuffled awkwardly. "Really . . . I just did—"

"Something *spectacular*," finished Blaster. "Now come on up here."

Unsure, the young giant hesitated. Then, drawing a deep breath, he made his way over to Blaster and clumsily climbed up beside him. Although it creaked under their weight, the platform held firm.

"Today," the mayor declared in a gravely serious tone, "I will greet you for the very first time with a traditional Giants' Salute. As you may know, this salute is given only to someone who has earned our very highest respect."

Placing his hands on the honoree's shoulders, he bellowed, "I salute you!" Then he raised his hands and slammed them down on those shoulders with great force.

Big Feet staggered, but with all his strength, kept himself from crumpling under the blow. The platform, however, wasn't so sturdy. Its wood cracked and burst apart, dropping both giants to the ground.

Almost everyone, including Big Feet, burst out laughing. But the mayor tried to retain a sense of decorum, even as he climbed back to his feet and brushed the debris off his belly. "Ahem," he said loudly. "Consider yourself saluted!"

The crowd released a unanimous cheer. "Well done, well done!" shouted several giants, raising their flasks of ale and half-eaten doughnuts. Even the toppled juggler got to his feet and cheered—before tripping on one of his garlics and falling down again.

"For giant-size bravery!" cried Sister, blowing the honoree a kiss. Unfortunately, in her excitement, she also sprayed slobber over several bystanders.

Catching Vonya's eye, Big Feet grinned broadly. She grinned back at him as her moist eyes reflected the firelight.

"Now," announced Blaster, "comes the most important part of the evening."

Turning to face his young companion, he declared, "By the power vested in me as your mayor, I will now reveal your true name. It is the name chosen by our elders this very afternoon."

All around the square, giants with gray or white hair

nodded solemnly. Some wore curly beards or flowing manes; others had lost most of their hair except for their eyebrows. Every one of them gazed at Big Feet with expressions of pride and admiration.

"Your name," the mayor continued, "comes from the giants' oldtongue—the ancient language of Fincayra's first people."

Big Feet stood his tallest . . . which was, indeed, impressively tall. He waited to hear his true name spoken aloud for the very first time.

"It is, of course, a relatively short name," said the mayor, "because of your relatively short time with us so far." He inhaled deeply and intoned: "Shimastimomolegavendernoodleterianoleeyami."

Pausing to take another breath, he added, "For everyday life . . . we'll just call you Shim."

Facing the crowd, he cried, "Let's hear it now for Shim!"

The crowd burst into thunderous cheers and applause. They threw hats, food, flasks of ale, and even a few boots into the night sky. "Shim!" they shouted merrily. "Here's to Shim!"

Finally, as the cheers died down, the mayor cleared

his throat. Never to be denied the final word, he declared, "This is a night of great joy for us all!"

"No," countered one lone voice, quavering but still loud enough to be heard. "No, it most certainly is not."

7.

DANCE OF THE GIANTS

The crowd of giants, so recently boisterous and joyful, fell completely silent. But for the steady crackle and snap of the bonfire, not a sound could be heard. Everyone, young and old, turned toward the speaker, an elderly giant who had only just arrived at the gathering.

Lunahlia, realized Shim. Like every other giant in Varigal, he recognized her—and watched in silence as she slowly made her way through the crowd, leaning heavily on her gnarled oaken staff. Her long white hair fell like a waterfall across her shoulders, glistening in the firelight. But more luminous still were her eyes, which shone like embers.

Lunahlia was one of the oldest giants alive. More importantly, she was a true seer. Often, she looked distracted, her mind watching scenes that had happened elsewhere in Fincayra . . . or that hadn't happened yet. The residents of Varigal, when confronted with something mysterious, would often say, "Only Lunahlia knows the truth."

Though Shim hadn't seen much of the seer, he had joined Vonya a few times when she'd visited Lunahlia's giantstone cottage on the farthest edge of the city. While the purpose of those visits had been to ask Lunahlia for help interpreting one of Vonya's dreams, Shim had always felt like something more was going on. Lunahlia had continually watched him, as if she was trying to assess his character. Or maybe read his future. No wonder he'd always been uncomfortable in her presence—and very glad when those visits had ended.

Now, as Lunahlia stepped into the center of the gathering, she raised her eyes. She looked directly at Shim—and scowled.

Meeting her gaze, he shuddered. Though he'd only

just been lauded for his bravery, he now felt weak in the knees.

For a long moment, she watched him, twirling a strand of white hair in her wrinkled hand. Then, to his surprise, she spoke to him telepathically, sending words right into his mind.

"Remember what you can of what I am about to say, young one." Lunahlia paused, twisting the tip of her staff into the stone pavement. *"But most of all . . . always remember that you really are a giant."*

Shim's mind whirled, trying to make sense of her message. Always remember that he's a giant? How could he possibly *not* remember that?

Lunahlia sighed, then turned to face the assembled giants. Her gaze, so often turned inward to see places and times far distant, clearly took in the scene here and now. Slowly, she scanned every expectant, worried face that surrounded her. At last, she spoke—and her words fell like a towering tree that slams down on the forest floor.

"We are doomed," she declared.

Murmurs of disbelief and moans of dismay rolled through the crowd. Vonya, for her part, strode over to join Shim. Placing her hefty hand on his shoulder, she whispered, "We're going to be all right, you and I."

As if in answer, Lunahlia declared, "Every last one of us is doomed, I tell you. Great evil and terrible troubles are upon us!"

She drew a long breath. "Some of those troubles have happened only recently, so recently that almost nobody knows about them. Others haven't happened yet, but will strike soon—very soon. All of these terrible tidings have come to me, just now, in visions that burned my mind like a fiery blaze."

Shaking, she leaned on her staff. "The first of our troubles—but not the last—is this: Tuatha, our great wizardking, is dead."

As one, the assembled giants gasped. Several of them cried out in pain, as if they had suddenly lost an eye or a limb.

"He died," she explained, "fighting to save us from yet another attack by the wicked warlord Gawr. And while Tuatha succeeded in banishing Gawr to the spirit realm, he himself perished, killed by one of the warlord's servants."

"Gone," wailed a young father holding a golden-haired infant in his arms. "Tuatha is gone!"

"Yes," said the seer grimly. "And worse, Tuatha's son

Stangmar, born without any magic of his own and envious of anyone who possesses it, has now taken the throne."

Above the swelling protests, she declared, "Everything I have said is true, coming from visions as clear as the breaking day. What I will say now, though, is less certain. For these visions are shrouded in mist."

Shim recalled the dreadful sight he'd seen earlier that day in the Living Mist. His body felt cold, making him shiver.

"Stangmar's remaining family has left him," continued Lunahlia. "Fearing for their lives, his wife, Elen, ran away with their son, a young boy with unusually promising magic. Where they have gone, I don't know . . . but I fear they may have left Fincayra forever."

"But no one can leave the island," protested a giant wearing a floppy hat made from woven cedar boughs. "They can't possibly pass through the Living Mist."

Gravely, she replied, "Probably true. Their only hope is that the young lad's magic is strong enough to guide and protect them. Yet he is awfully young and untested. He isn't at all aware of his powers, let alone his destiny."

She glanced over at Shim. Speaking slowly and quietly, she added, "All we can do is hope that he will somehow survive the many ordeals to come."

On his shoulder, Shim felt Vonya's grip tighten.

Lunahlia shook her head morosely. "Even Stangmar's mother, Olwen, has fled. And Fincayra is much less without dear Olwen! I have known her for many years, starting way back when she was the beautiful merwoman courted by Tuatha. So great was her love for him that she left her people as well as her ancestral home in the sea just to be with him, trading her fish tail for human legs. And now . . . I have no idea where she could go, or how she could ever find a home."

"Ohhh," moaned Shim. "That's so verily sad." All around him, giants nodded in agreement.

"There is more, I fear." Keeping one hand on her staff, Lunahlia twisted a strand of her hair with the other. "Even though he was banished to the realm of the spirits, Gawr still has ways to reach Stangmar—and to bend the new king to his will. Stangmar's anger runs deep, and his resentment of magic runs even deeper, making him easily corrupted."

She paused, grimacing. "I have learned that Gawr has convinced Stangmar to assemble an army of undead warriors—the ghoulliants. Together with their allies the gobsken, they have started work on the ancient temple of

Lorilanda, built long ago over the sacred spring of Eagles Canyon. Their goal is to transform it into a fortress. Yes—a dreadful castle that will turn constantly on its foundation, shrouded by dark fumes. Soon the Shrouded Castle will be feared by all Fincayrans."

"Terrible," muttered Blaster, so crestfallen that his voice was barely audible. "Truly terrible."

"There is still more," said Lunahlia ominously. "Stangmar has ordered his agents to search for the famous Treasures of Fincayra, our island's most powerful magical objects. This very day, I believe, his loyalists stole several of them from people who have guarded them devotedly for centuries—including the Flowering Harp, whose music can bring springtime to devastated places; the sword Deepercut, which can slice into anyone's soul; and the Wise Plow, which can till its own field forever. What he plans to do with these great Treasures and any others he can find . . . I have no idea."

The midwife Gargolyn shook her head, shaking her ropes of gray hair. "Whatever he's planning, it can't be good."

Shim glanced over at the bonfire, now burning much lower than before, its flames darkening as its coals grew steadily dimmer. Drawing a deep breath, he told himself,

We giants will be fine. Nobody, even undead warriors, can harm us.

Lunahlia's head snapped around instantly, and she gave him a sharp look—as if she knew exactly what he had thought. After a moment, she continued.

"On top of all this . . . my visions included a prophecy. It reveals the one and only weakness of the Shrouded Castle—and what could be its demise."

Her voice dropped lower and she chanted:

> *Where in darkness a castle doth spin,*
> *Small will be large, ends will begin.*
> *Only when giants make dance in the hall*
> *Shall every barrier crumble and fall.*

"What does it mean?" asked Vonya, her hand still clasping Shim's shoulder. "What does it mean for us, for our people?"

Lunahlia gazed at her soulfully. Finally, she said, "I believe that others, too, have heard this prophecy—the great bard Cairpré, the sorceress Elusa in her Crystal Cave . . . and also, unfortunately, Stangmar. They are calling it the Dance of the Giants, for it says that only giants can destroy the evil castle. Only when we dance within its walls—"

"*Shall every barrier,*" completed Vonya, "*crumble and fall.*"

"That's great," yelled Lumpster, pumping his fists in the air. "Let's go trash that castle!"

The seer glared at him. "Not so fast! If you tried, just once, to think with your brains instead of your biceps, you'd see that we have a much bigger problem."

Shim stiffened as he realized the truth. "Stangmar! Would he try to attack us?"

"Maybe he'll imprison us," called someone in the crowd.

"Let him try!" answered another giant. "We're bigger and stronger than any of his warriors."

"Don't be a fool," shouted a different giant. "Stangmar's warriors are deadly, even to us! That's how they killed—"

"My husband," finished Vonya. Her hand on Shim's shoulder trembled with emotion. "Jonkl was one of our biggest and bravest." She swallowed. "And we still lost him."

Reaching up, Shim placed his own hand over hers. Gently, he squeezed, trying to say without any words what she most needed to hear. In response, she gave him a look of gratitude.

"What will Stangmar do?" several giants asked at once. "What are his plans?"

Lunahlia's bright eyes surveyed the crowd. "I have just seen his plans in my visions. They spring from his fear of our strength—and also his fear that we alone, as this island's first people, could rally other Fincayran races to rebel against him."

She raised her staff and angrily slammed it against the stone at her feet, so hard that sparks flew into the air. "The sparks of his fears have been fanned into flames by the wicked Gawr. And now the prophecy has thrown fuel on those flames. So Stangmar's plans are . . ."

She drew a slow, halting breath before continuing. "To kill us. To kill us all!"

Over the giants' cries of outrage and disbelief, she raised her voice to shout, "My people, hear me! We must all leave Varigal at once. Flee into the hills—find somewhere, anywhere, to hide."

"No!" objected several giants, Blaster among them. "We must fight!" he bellowed. "Giants don't run and hide. Stand and defend our great city!"

"If you do, you will perish," declared Lunahlia with finality. "In the terrible times we are soon to enter . . .

anyone who looks like a giant will surely die."

"Anyone who looks like a giant?" asked Vonya desperately. "Then we have no chance!"

"Unless," the elder replied, "you can find some way to hide. Either that, or transform into something else— which is impossible."

Vonya caught her breath. Suddenly possessed by a wild idea, she squeezed Shim's shoulder all the harder.

"Go now, I say!" cried Lunahlia. "Save yourselves so that someday, Fincayra's most ancient and honorable people will rise again!"

The gathering in the market square dissolved into a frenzied panic. Some giants ran to their homes to collect their children or their most precious belongings. Others surrounded Blaster, vowing to fight whatever foes dared to attack. Still others chose to flee immediately, grabbing hold of their loved ones and hurtling toward one of the city's exits. Vonya, in the latter group, took Shim's hand and pulled him toward the main gates.

Too late!

With ear-piercing shrieks and howls, the attack on Varigal began.

8.

THE RIVER UNCEASING

Like a fatal flood, the army of Stangmar poured through the main gates of Varigal. Hollow-eyed ghoulliants, whose decomposing flesh still clung to their faces and hands, shrieked angrily as they threw themselves headlong at the giants, piercing their prey with poisoned spears. Gobsken warriors charged right behind, their green arms bulging with muscles as they brandished their heavy broadswords. Wearing iron breastplates and pointed helmets, they formed groups of six or more and methodically used their swords to wound and kill any giants they met.

Howls of terror and shrieks of rage echoed in the market square and the surrounding streets. Where jovial merriment had filled the air moments before, only the clamor of battle could now be heard. As the giants fought for their lives, food tables collapsed and broke apart. Statues of generations of ancestors toppled, splintering into thousands of shards. Hats, ribbons, and colorful vests lay strewn across the square, trampled by careless boots. The city's streets, once sparkling white giantstone, turned the color of blood.

Before long, Stangmar's forces overwhelmed the last of their foes. Giants old and young lay lifeless, their once-powerful bodies brutally beaten or dismembered. While some of them had fought supremely well, taking many gobsken lives, they had ultimately succumbed. The giants' capital city was now a graveyard.

Among the dead lay the seer Lunahlia. Her once-bright eyes gazed lifelessly at the night sky, no longer viewing this time and place . . . or any other.

After a last murderous search for any more giants, the ghoulliants and gobsken marched out of the city's gates. They carried tokens of their great victory—a giant's severed hand, a glittering jewel that had been someone's amulet, a scrap of silk from a scarf that had been a treasured family heirloom.

Most satisfying of all, the warriors knew beyond any doubt that no giants had survived. Their master—and the spirit warlord who guided him—would be greatly pleased to hear that the giants' threat to their plans had been completely eliminated.

But they were wrong.

As the first rays of sunrise touched Fincayra, dark red hues seeped into the lands surrounding the ruins of Varigal. Only an eagle soaring high overhead could have spied the two hulking forms who now clambered across a boulder field at the northernmost edge of the Misted Hills.

Vonya and Shim moved swiftly, just as they'd done since barely escaping through a hidden gate that Vonya had remembered. Sometimes they leaped across crevasses, other times they stepped over boulders big enough to crush a whole family of humans. Whatever the obstacles, they never paused—not even for a drink of water from a surging stream.

"When can we stop?" asked Shim, his face red in the dawn light. "I'm as thirstily as a thousand fishes."

Vonya glanced over her shoulder at him and frowned. "Not yet, Big F—I mean Shim. We must keep going east until we're far, far away from these hills."

Catching one of his hairy toes on a fallen tree, Shim stumbled. "But . . ."

"Later, my jelly roll."

"Where are we going, anyway?"

"Later."

She sped up the pace—not so fast they couldn't stay together, but fast enough to make talking difficult. And to bring them nearer to their destination. In this dire moment, every instant counted.

For several more hours they pushed on. Shim's legs ached from walking, his throat screamed for water, and he felt sleepier than ever before in his life. But he bravely kept marching. What he'd seen of last night's terrible attack was more than enough motivation. That—and his bottomless well of trust in his mother. If she could summon the strength to keep going . . . well, then so could he.

Despite his good intentions, though, he started to falter. More and more often, he tripped on logs or stones, even on small branches. Once he accidentally stepped into a pit of sleeping vipers, waking them in a fit of angry hisses and coiled bodies. He jumped away just in time, tearing his leggings in the process.

Finally, when his legs were just about to collapse under him, they reached a mighty river. Sheltered by a steep-walled canyon that rose up twice his height, and bordered by a thick tangle of willows and cottonwoods, this river was a safe place to rest and recover. And to drink!

Shim sat on the bank and plunged his whole head into the tumbling current, gulping down as much water as he could hold. Vonya, meanwhile, sat down beside him. For several heartbeats, she simply watched him, grateful that they had survived the most horrible night of their lives—and of their people's entire history. Since the day long ago when the great spirit Dagda had carved the first giants from a mountainside, nothing as calamitous as this had ever befallen them.

Where, she wondered, was Dagda now, when they needed him most? Was he battling against that wicked warlord Gawr, now banished to the spirit realm? If so . . . was Dagda joined by the spirit of her beloved Jonkl in that battle?

Taking a deep drink from the river, she felt sure of

the answer. *Jonkl is fighting for what's right and good, that much I know.* She raised her face, now wet from river water as well as her own tears. *And I promise you, my dear heart . . . I will never stop doing the same.*

"Ahhh," sighed Shim as he lifted his head from the flowing water. "Now that's a real drink! Certainly and waterly."

Looking down the river, he noticed some oval-shaped boulders that seemed perfectly rounded. Too perfectly, in fact. Almost as if they were actually something else.

"Tell me," he said, pointing at the boulders. "Are those big smoothish stones over there really . . . eggs?"

Slowly, she nodded. "Yes. Very observant of you." Reaching over, she took his hand. "But that's a story that must wait for another time."

"All rightly." He shook his head, spraying her with water. "At least, though, tell me where we are now."

"I will. But not until I tell you how proud I am of my son. That was a very rough night, but you kept going."

"Of coursely!" He gave her a nudge. "Isn't that what a grownupish person would do?"

She nodded sadly. "Yes, it is. But nobody, child or grown-up, should have to experience what we did last night."

A wave of grief washed over both of them. Colder and more penetrating than river water, it soaked them to the marrow of their bones.

Shim grimaced. Where were all their friends, their neighbors, their elders, like Lunahlia? Gone—all gone. And where were the statue-lined streets of Varigal, so rich with history and tradition? Gone. And all those simple things he'd known his entire life—the sound of laughter in the market square, the smell of roasting ubermushrooms, the warmth of a crackling hearth fire in their cottage? Gone.

"Do you think," he asked hoarsely, "anyone else survived the attack?"

"I don't know. I pray to Dagda and Lorilanda that some people did . . . but I don't know."

For a long moment, they didn't speak. They just sat there together on the bank, listening to the rushing river. At last, Vonya said, "At least we made it here, you and I."

"And where is here?"

"Not far from the headwaters of the River Unceasing, the big river that runs right down the middle of this island. To the west, where we came from, is our . . ." She paused to swallow before saying the word. "Home. And many special places, like the Druma Wood, so rich with natural magic that its trees can actually talk."

Shim's eyes widened. "Really? Talking trees?"

"Yes. And over there," she said with a wave to the east, "lie the plains, Eagles Canyon, and soon . . . that dreadful castle you heard about last night."

Gravely, he nodded. "The one that will smoke and spin and hold the new king."

"Stangmar. And his murderous warriors."

Shim furrowed his brow, trying to understand. "So why would we ever want to go there, to such a horribobilous place?"

"We're not going to the Shrouded Castle," she assured him. "But we needed to go this way to reach the place where we *are* going. A place, I'm afraid, that's . . . well . . . even worse."

"What?" The young giant sitting beside her jumped, nearly sliding into the river. "Do you really mean that?"

"I do," she said gravely. Pausing to choose the best words to describe her plan, she listened to the constant whooshing of the water. Finally, she explained, "We must go to . . . the Haunted Marsh."

"What?" he sputtered. "Why would we ever want to do *that*?"

"Because that's where we might find the sorceress Domnu. She is terribly unreliable . . . and in her own way, even more dangerous than the Haunted Marsh. But she is the only person on this whole island who might possibly have enough magic to help you. To keep you safe! With Tuatha gone and Stangmar on the throne . . . she is our only hope."

Utterly baffled, Shim stood up and waded into the river. Dunking his head again, he shook himself wildly and rubbed his fingers into his ears. As he returned to the bank, dripping wet, he shook himself again before sitting back down.

"There," he said with relief. "I needed to rinse out my cloggily ears! I thought you said we need to go to a truly dangerous, haunted swamp . . . to find an even more dangerous sorceress . . . who might possibly help us if she doesn't kill us first."

Vonya peered at him sadly. "That's right."

"What? Motherly, have you lost your mind?"

"Maybe," she replied, slumping dejectedly. "And yet . . . I can't think of any other way to save you from Stangmar."

"We can hide, can't we? Go someplace so secretish that he'll never find us."

"There is no such place, Shim. Remember what Lunahlia said before the attack? Anyone who looks like a giant will surely die."

"But we'll die if we do this crazily thing!"

"Maybe so, my dearest." She inhaled a long, uncertain breath. "Or maybe not. Which is why we have to try."

For a long moment, Shim peered at her, chewing his lip. Finally, he declared, "Whereverly you go, I'll go."

9.

FLOWERS OF PEACE

Together, the intrepid pair crossed the river and climbed out of its canyon. Leaving that shelter behind, they found themselves exposed to the wind that often whipped across the grassy plains. Sometimes it blew so hard that Shim or Vonya lost their balance, grabbing the other's arm for support.

One of those howling gusts nearly knocked both of them over. To keep moving, they hunched their massive bodies down closer to the ground. Vonya's hair rope, so recently decorated with white pelican feathers, had long since fallen free, so her auburn hair blew in the direction of the wind. And Shim's always-wild mane looked even more frenzied than usual, blown in all directions like the radiating spines of an enormous sea urchin.

At a lull, he asked, "Who could possibly live in this windsilly place?"

"Dwarves," replied Vonya. "But they live in caverns down under the ground. So they're rarely seen by anyone."

"What are dwarves? I've neverly heard of them."

She waited for another gust to die down before responding. "They're little people. Very little. About knee-high on a human."

Shim gave a compassionate sigh. "Poor them, being so smallsy. I'm very glad to be a giant . . . even on such a windywild day!"

He didn't notice Vonya's frown.

For the rest of that morning, they trekked eastward across the plains. While they met no creatures bigger than a tan-colored hare who hopped across their path, they saw abundant tracks of antelope as well as dagger-claw bear.

Finally, when the sun was high overhead, they came to a deep ravine carved by a stream flowing out of the

Dark Hills. Vonya proposed they stay the rest of the day in that spot, hidden by the ravine's shadowed walls from the wind—and also from sight. Shim didn't object. In fact, after a good drink from the stream, he quickly propped himself against the bank and fell fast asleep.

Vonya, meanwhile, kept watch. Suddenly, she heard gruff voices and heavy boots approaching. Peeking over the eroded edge of the ravine, she spied a troop of gobsken, armed with spears and broadswords, marching across the plains. Completely motionless, she watched them pass, fighting back her fears . . . as well as her rage. She wanted to burst out of hiding and stomp every last one of them into dust! But she resisted. For she knew that her life now had just one purpose: to save her child.

She watched the gobsken depart, vowing to succeed somehow.

When the sun, at last, fell below the horizon, dusk cloaked the world in shadows. She roused Shim from his slumber—no easy feat. Then, side by side, they left the ravine and continued their trek.

Bearing south to avoid the gobsken, they marched in silence. With nightfall, the winds lessened considerably, making it much easier to walk. Like two hulking shadows that had materialized out of the deepening dusk, they strode across the plains. But for the endless trill of crickets, and the distant howl of a wolf, they heard no sounds.

Sometime during the night, they smelled smoke from campfires. Fearing a gobsken encampment, Vonya led them as far away as possible until the smoke dissipated. Heading south again, they passed near a human settlement from which they could hear strains of lovely music. Some people played on harps and flutes, while others sang soulfully.

Caer Neithen, realized Vonya, *the place people call Town of the Bards.*

Knowing that the town was the home of the great poet Cairpré, she felt tempted to veer over there and tell him all about the giants' peril. But she held back, aware of the risks. Stangmar could have spies there, even in a place where music and scholarship ruled. Besides . . . a bard as wise as Cairpré probably already knew about the fate of Varigal, perhaps from his conversations with a soaring eagle or with one of those invisible wind sisters, beings who had flown high above Fincayra for almost as long as giants had walked upon its surface.

As dawn began to brighten the sky, they smelled something rancid in the air—a revolting mix of stagnant water, rotten wood, and decomposing flesh. As the stench grew steadily stronger, they knew they were approaching their destination.

Less than an hour later, they stood at the edge of the Haunted Marsh. The ground underfoot felt moist, even mushy. Ahead of them, dead trees stood in puddles of oozing murk. Distant shrieks and moans wafted out of the dark fog that encircled the skeletal trees and smothered the surrounding land.

Shim set his hand on Vonya's shoulder. His voice just a whisper, he asked, "Are you sure this is a goodly idea?"

A spine-tingling shriek, from somewhere out there in the putrid fog, made him start. "This place feels shiverishly haunted."

Vonya turned toward him, her feet squelching in the muck. "Listen to me. We won't know if this is a good idea or a bad one until we try."

She waved away a flock of bats who flew past her face. "But I can tell you this: The Haunted Marsh isn't entirely what it seems."

"What do you mean?"

"Long ago," she explained, "this place wasn't a smelly bog at all. It was a vast meadowland, full of beautiful flowers and delicious fruits. Trees blossomed, birds sang, and colorful butterflies danced among the flowers."

Shim frowned in disbelief. "Really? Are you sure?"

She nodded. "Giants have long memories. And I remember hearing my dear grandpa tell me about how this place looked long ago . . . which he'd heard described by his own grandfather."

Still not convinced, Shim scanned the fetid landscape. Strange shapes, some that seemed almost aglow, moved through the fog. "If that's true, then something awfullous must have happened here."

"It did. You see, a community of women also lived here. Women of magic. They called themselves the Xania-Soe, which in the oldtongue means *Flowers of Peace*. For many years, they studied these meadows, learning how to coax powerful perfumes from the flowers—scents that could be used for healing and creating. But the magic of those flowers was strong. If used wrongly, it could also be made to destroy other forms of life."

She paused, still hearing the wonder—and the fear—in her grandpa's voice as he described what came next.

"So powerful was the work of the Xania-Soe, even the wind refused to blow through this region. That was the only way to prevent such dangerous knowledge from spreading elsewhere . . . and falling into evil hands. Hands that would seek not to heal, but to destroy."

A round of terrifying shrieks, from deep in the fog, halted her. Protectively, Shim slid his arm through hers.

"Eventually, the secret power of this place was discovered by a terrible warlord bent on conquering the entire island. An ancestor of our own evil Gawr. He tried to conquer the Flowers of Peace and steal their great knowledge—and he almost succeeded."

"What happened?"

"Just when the evil army was about to invade and the women knew that all hope was lost, they made a terrible sacrifice. To repel the invaders, they threw a curse on their beloved homeland—a curse that made their magical flowers spew poisonous vapors into the air. Those very poisons seeped into the land itself, twisting all life into death, all light into shadow. Despite all their rage and grief, the women refused to leave their longtime home. Soon, they transformed into deadly, ghastly beings—the marsh ghouls."

Shim's whole body stiffened. "So this place really is verily haunted!"

"It is, yes. The marsh ghouls are all that's left of that once-marvelous community. And they continue to guard their territory. They feel only sorrow and rage, I'm afraid . . . and they take deadly revenge on anyone who dares to enter."

"Which is what you want us to do! Motherly, you is full of madness!"

She heaved a heavy sigh. "I suppose you're right. I *am* full of madness . . . at least when it comes to saving you."

"So we really must go in there?"

"Yes, we must. It's no accident the sorceress Domnu chose to live in the middle of this frightful place. She wants only visitors who are truly desperate, who will give everything they have for her help."

Shim shuddered. No telling which was worse—the ghouls, the swamp, or the sorceress. "Do you truly want to do this?"

Peering deep into his eyes, she asked, "Knowing everything I've told you . . . do *you?*"

He gazed back at her. Finally, he said, "Whereverly you go . . . I'll go."

"All right, then."

They faced the Haunted Marsh, where voices shrieked and wailed, poisonous fumes drifted, and shapeless forms floated. Then, arm in arm, they entered it together.

10.

MARSH GHOULS

A reeking smell, like festering fish, drifted over the two giants as they plodded deeper into the swamp. Their enormous bare feet squelched noisily in the muck. Arm in arm, they kept walking, even as the fog darkened around them.

Meanwhile, the wailing and shrieking cries swelled louder. One high, thin voice in particular made Shim's skin crawl. Heavy with suffering, it came from someone keening in anguish.

Suddenly, Vonya halted, making Shim also stop. Off to one side appeared a faint, wavering light . . . as eerie as the vague glow they'd seen earlier, but more intense. The light hovered in the darkness, shrouded by swirling vapors. It seemed, somehow, to be watching them. A marsh ghoul!

Another eerie light appeared, floating right in front of them. Then another, and another. Before long, a dozen or more lights glowed ominously, wavering and watching.

"Let's keep going," said Vonya. Trying to sound more confident than she felt, she added, "Maybe the ghouls won't harm us."

Slowly, they trudged ahead. The wailing voices grew louder, like a pack of wolves surrounding their prey. With every step, the muck smelled more rancid, assaulting their noses and throats, even as it oozed between their toes and clung to their ankles.

All the while . . . the lights circled, drawing ever closer. Reflected in pools of slime, the lights flickered rhythmically. Sometimes they flared with sudden brightness. Shim felt sure the ghouls were communicating with each other, plotting their attack.

"Aaaarrgh!" cried Vonya as she stepped off a ledge into a deep pool. She pitched forward, losing her grip on Shim. As she splashed down, she sank steadily deeper into the muck.

"No!" shouted Shim. Panic exploded in his mind, making him freeze.

Then, unexpectedly, he felt a surge of strength, pushing aside the panic. *Help her! Must help her!* She couldn't be far away. Maybe still within reach.

Guided by the sound of her cries for help and her wild flailing, he fell to his knees. Creeping as close as he dared to the edge of the pool, he reached forward, feeling for her. "Come to me," he shouted. "I'm right here!"

Her flailing continued. She coughed violently, spitting out ooze that she'd swallowed. Though Shim knew she was somewhere close, he couldn't see her in the gloom. But he reached out even farther—for in just a few more seconds, she could drown.

"I'm right here! Let me help you!"

Her hand! It slapped against his wrist, clasping tight. He grabbed her with his other hand and tugged mightily.

At first, she didn't budge. Her continued flailing seemed only to drag her down deeper. And then . . . she moved a bit nearer to him.

Shim pulled harder. The muscles on his back and arms and legs burned painfully. But he barely noticed. Nothing was going to stop him now—nothing at all.

Finally, with a sudden lurch and a loud *thhhwucckk*, she reached the edge beside him. Weakly, she crawled higher as he pulled her out of the pool.

Together, they leaned against each other, panting heavily in the darkness. Although Vonya coughed some more, she seemed uninjured. Shim, meanwhile, felt satisfied just to know that she was there with him again.

As all this was happening, the marsh ghouls' wailing cries grew more frenzied. At the same time, their eerie lights pressed closer. They floated right above the huddled giants, as well as on every side . . . as if all they wanted to do was cause more suffering, more anguish, more loss.

Jumping to his feet, Shim shouted into the gloom. "Stop harassing us, you wickedly persons! We didn't come to this place for your murkish madness. We came here for some help!"

The voices shrieked angrily, unused to such treatment. Wild howlings swelled along with snarls and moans. Simultaneously, the lights flashed intensely, surging closer.

Shim, though, paid no heed. With his mother slumped beside him, still coughing from her ordeal, he burned with righteous indignation.

"Back off!" he cried, raising his muddy fists at the marsh ghouls. "I know you're angry because you lost your homes and your families. Well, so did we! Just yesterday—we lost everything and everyone!"

The wailing cries abruptly ceased. Meanwhile, the floating lights dimmed and pulled a little farther away.

"We're the only giants left," he called into the fetid air. "My mother and me! She almost died just now . . . and you don't care a bit. Don't you know what it's like to have a mother? A loved one? A somelybody you'd do anything to save?"

The lights drew back even more. But Shim wasn't yet finished.

"Go back to your ghoulishness. Just leave us alone! So we can find that wicked sorceress who will maybily help us."

Roaring into the darkness, he added, "Go now! Go away! Just like you would if you was still the same as long ago—peaceful and magical and lovelyish. If you was still . . . Flowers of Peace."

Instantly, the lights went out, their glowing extinguished. Cast into complete darkness, the giants couldn't see anything. All they could hear was their own ragged breathing, the occasional cough, and the pounding of their hearts. But at least . . . they still had each other.

Wobbling, Vonya regained her feet. She wrapped both arms, dripping with muck, around her son. Gladly, he hugged her back.

Though darkness blanketed them, she knew just where to find his ear. And into it she whispered, "Like I told you before, you know the most important thing about being a giant."

"I do?"

"Yes, my jelly roll, you do." She cleared her throat. "Bigness means more than the size of your bones."

For the first time, he caught at least a hint of the meaning in those words.

Suddenly—the marsh ghouls' light returned, glowing brighter than before. Yet instead of surrounding the two bedraggled giants . . . they now formed a long, serpentine line of light that led across the marsh, stretching far into the distance. A radiant pathway.

Then, to the shock of Shim and Vonya, they noticed something else: Beneath the glowing lights of the marsh ghouls, flowers bloomed. As brightly colored as the surrounding swamp was bland, the flowers lined the luminous path.

Without any words, the two giants started walking. Stepping in unison through the flowers, they followed the path around bottomless pits, sharp ledges, and dead trees—as well as the shadowed lairs of beings that hissed or growled as they passed. Yet even amidst such dangerous surroundings, they knew beyond doubt that they would now survive crossing the marsh.

For this wondrous pathway was a gift. A gift from the Flowers of Peace.

II.

NO TURNING BACK

Wearily, the two mud-crusted giants trudged for several hours across the Haunted Marsh. Guided by the luminous, flowering pathway of the marsh ghouls, they avoided the various death traps that would otherwise have ended their trek . . . and their lives. Even so, both Shim and Vonya felt continually oppressed by the rancid, stifling air of the swamp. It stung their eyes and burned their lungs, making them both miss the clean mountain air of Varigal. Even the relentless, howling wind of the plains was preferable to this fetid fog!

Something else oppressed them: the grave dangers

of visiting Domnu. The sorceress, Vonya explained, had lived on Fincayra nearly as long as the entire race of the giants. Not that she'd feel any compulsion to help them because of the longevity she shared with their kind. To the contrary, legends told that she felt no loyalty at all to anyone else—not even Dagda in the spirit realm. As an ancient hag who had seen hundreds of generations of mortals come and go, she viewed all other creatures and their troubles with complete disinterest.

Unless they could, somehow, be of use to her. That was the only hope of striking a bargain with Domnu. And it wasn't just a faint hope—it was a terribly danger- ous one. For she had no concerns at all about morality. Right and wrong meant nothing to her.

Appropriately, the meaning of her name in the old-tongue was *Dark Fate*. Maybe that arose from her famous penchant for gambling, for games where fate or chance held sway. Or maybe it just meant that she cared nothing at all about anyone's life except her own.

As the bard Cairpré had written in a ballad about Domnu: "She is not good or evil, friend or foe, mortal or immortal. She simply *is*."

That thin sliver of hope that the hag might need

something—something that a fully grown giant like Vonya could provide—was the entire basis of her desperate plan. A weak basis, to be sure. But it was the only way that Vonya could possibly get the hag to use her magic to protect Shim. Otherwise . . . her son would never survive to adulthood. Not in this era of the malicious, brutal King Stangmar.

Of course, Vonya hadn't yet revealed the details of her plan to Shim. He would certainly protest mightily and try to stop her. But she felt such a strong protective instinct for him that she was prepared to deal with his objections when the time came. And she knew that once they entered Domnu's lair, there would be no turning back.

The radiant path veered around a series of pits that were bubbling ominously, as if the ooze within them was constantly aboil. Or perhaps it was actually one connected pit that boiled in several places. Either way, the giants felt very glad indeed to avoid that stretch of swamp.

Abruptly, they stopped. Not far ahead, swathed in dark fumes, rose a towering shape, at least three times the height of Vonya. It could have been a huge, rocky pinnacle—but its shape looked almost like some sort of building. A ramshackle, topsy-turvy, precariously made building.

Then the fog shifted, revealing a row of barred windows near the top—removing all doubt. From behind the windows, amber light glowed. Was it the light of a fireplace? Or of some eerie magic?

"What a messy, hovelly place," said Shim. "All piled with rocks and dead trees and . . ." He paused to gulp. "Bones! Errr . . . do you thinks she really lives there?"

Vonya nodded grimly. "That's her lair, all right. Though it looks like it could cave in at any moment."

"Why would anybody want to live in such a ramshackelous place?"

Her voice grave, Vonya answered, "To keep away visitors."

"Like us."

"Yes, like us."

Shifting his gaze to the pathway, Shim noticed something else. "The ghoulsy lights—they end right over there, in front of the building."

"So there's no doubt," said Vonya grimly. "That's Domnu's lair."

Even as she spoke, the marsh ghouls' lights started

to change. In unison, they grew dimmer and less steady, wavering eerily as they had done when Shim and Vonya first entered the bog. Meanwhile, the moaning and wailing sounds resumed, making the air feel, once again, heavy with anguish.

Listening to the marsh ghouls' heartrending cries, Shim frowned compassionately. Their pain seemed to claw at his heart. He called to them—and the moment he started to speak, the wailing stopped again.

"Thank you, peaceful flower ghouls. Thank you verily much!"

Opening his arms wide, he added gently, "I am so sorry for all your losses, all your pain. Deeply and achingly sorry."

For a long moment, the swamp remained quiet. Except for the bubbling of the pits and the hissing of a snake, there were no sounds.

Then, as one, the marsh ghouls began to cry and moan, just as they had before. The flowers lining the path melted away, vanishing without a trace. As if blown by a mysterious wind, the ghouls scattered widely. Vaporous veils shrouded their lights so that the fog glowed ominously all around.

Vonya touched her son's forearm. "What you said was beautiful."

"Just speaking truly, that's all."

She touched his face, gently running her fingers over his cheek. At last, she asked, "Do you trust me?"

Surprised, he nodded. "Of coursely I do."

"Then . . . I want you to promise me something. Whatever I need to do to convince Domnu to help you survive—you will cooperate. No matter how terrible or evil it sounds—you will do whatever I need you to do."

He scrunched his nose. *Whatever?*"

"Whatever."

With a heavy sigh, he said, "All rightly. I promise."

She gave his arm a squeeze. "Then I will have the strength to go through with this."

Shim cocked his head thoughtfully. "You really is full of madness!"

Almost grinning, she replied, "Yes, I am."

"And so is I. Certainly, definitely, absolutely."

Together, they strode toward the lair of the sorceress whose name meant *Dark Fate*.

12.

DOMNU

E ven getting to the lair, which truly deserved Shim's
word *ramshackelous*, wasn't easy. Without the marsh
ghouls, deep darkness shrouded everything except the
ominous glow from the lair's windows. Making matters
worse, there was so much rubble, including rock slabs
and uprooted trees, blocking the entrance path that even
the long-legged giants had trouble crossing over. Only
the fact that this route looked more passable than the
gurgling pits on both sides made it a path at all.

Like the building itself, the jumble of barriers on the
path fairly shouted: *Perilous! Dangerous! Turn back now!*

Exactly as Domnu wanted.

More unnerving to Shim and Vonya, though, were all the bones. Thousands and thousands of bones lay in huge piles around the lair. They were the remains of countless legs, arms, feet, wings, tails, and vertebrae, and they reeked of suffering and death. Seeing them, it wasn't hard to imagine the life force that had once made them move with strength and grace. For good measure, a long line of skulls—from bears, humans, wolves, horses, and at least one giant—bordered the outer wall of the lair.

Set in the center of the building's front wall, at the very end of the path, gaped the opening of a tunnel. There wasn't any door, or any indication of what might lurk inside. Just a frighteningly dark hole.

Vonya led the way. Bending over to fit through the tunnel, she waved for Shim to follow. Reluctantly, he came behind her, already regretting his promise to do whatever she asked him to do.

They trudged through the tunnel, scraping their massive shoulders on the rough-hewn stones above them. With every step, amber light grew stronger. But it wasn't the warm, welcoming light of someone's home—more like the dim, shimmering light from dying fire coals.

We are full of madness, Shim said anxiously to himself. Entering this place felt terribly dangerous. Certainly, dreadfully, absolutely.

Finally, they pushed open a heavy door that had been left ajar . . . as if their arrival had been expected. Together, they entered a cavernous room with a high ceiling. Glancing overhead, Shim saw some furry creature scurry along one of the rotting beams and disappear into a dark corner. Just then, a slab of stone that had been wedged under the beam broke off and fell to the floor, smashing into bits only an arm's length from the giants.

"Whoa!" shouted Shim, leaping aside. "This place is even more rickety and crickety than I thought."

Vonya nodded worriedly. "Let's just hope it lasts long enough for us to do what we have to do."

Peering at her inquisitively, Shim asked, "And what exactishly is that?"

Another scurrying—this one right by their feet— made them both jump. Something darted past, vanishing into the shadows, leaving no trace except a dank, musty smell that lingered like smoke. Other smells, too, assaulted their sensitive nostrils—all of them rancid. The lair smelled like an ancient cave that had never been cleaned of dead bodies, garbage, and defecation.

As they scanned the enormous room, both of them realized that the amber light didn't have any visible source—no candles, torches, or hearths. Only the eerie, shifting glow that hung in the air.

All around them sat piles of strange objects. Some, like a set of wooden blocks that had been stacked in the shape of a pyramid, were carefully organized. Others, like a collection of polished stones etched with mysterious runes, lay jumbled haphazardly. Spools of yarn, black and white and red, filled several huge baskets. Gaping iron bowls held seashells, jewels, small bones, seeds, crystal spheres, painted cards, and what looked like bundles of human hair.

One bowl, set beside a shadowy doorway, held something more ominous—eyeballs. Dozens and dozens of eyeballs, wet and glistening. Seeing them, Shim winced.

The nearest wall, made from smooth slabs of rock, showed countless markings. Columns of blue slashes bled into rows of yellow dots and purple squiggles. Squares, pentagons, triangles, circles, and arrows filled every available space. Scrawled between these markings, and sometimes over them, were thousands more runes, numbers, and some weirdly glowing symbols.

By the opposite wall sat a large, hairy rug divided into red and black squares. It looked like the chess board that Shim and Vonya had seen in the cottage of Lunahlia . . . but hers was much smaller. As were her chess pieces— these were each as big as a tree trunk. And instead of standard shapes, these pieces looked like animals from all around Fincayra: horses, sea lions, monkeys, a pair of fiery red dragons, and one lone unicorn.

As he looked closely at the animals, Shim caught the slightest quiver of the unicorn's white mane. Then, so quietly that it could barely be heard, the creature made a tiny noise—part neigh, part whimper. As if in response, one of the dragons crinkled its wing ever so slightly, flared its nostrils, and blew a small puff of smoke.

"By the beard of Dagda," exclaimed Shim. "Those chessly pieces are alive!"

Before Vonya could respond, a new voice growled from the room's darkest corner. "Alive or dead . . . what does it matter? It's all the same to me."

Both giants stiffened as, from deep in the shadows, Domnu emerged. The hairless head of the sorceress glistened in the amber light, her scalp so wrinkled it resembled an exposed brain. A large wart protruded like a horn from her forehead, while her eyes, as black as a moonless night, studied her guests, never blinking.

Swishing her tan robe, which held several bulging pockets, she stepped toward the giants. She paused to examine them more closely, taking in everything from their bushy heads down to their bare feet. All the while she stared at them, unblinking, as she fingered her necklace of clear quartz crystals.

"Well, well," she growled, her mouth full of misshapen teeth. "This is truly a pleasure. And believe me, at my age I am rarely pleased about anything."

Vonya started to speak, but the ancient hag cut her off. "Let me guess why you're here, my pets. Running away from Stangmar's warriors, perhaps?"

The giants both gasped.

Domnu reached up to scratch her wrinkled brow. "Or are you already hoping to fulfill the new prophecy? The Dance of the Giants?"

Vonya and Shim traded nervous glances, amazed that she knew so much.

"Not that it matters," continued Domnu with a shrug. "Life. Death. It makes no difference at all."

"But it does," Shim countered passionately. "Most absolutely, it does!"

She regarded him harshly. "Not to me, it doesn't."

Vonya motioned to Shim to stay quiet. But he ignored her and demanded, "Why are you so grumpy and crumbumbly? We came here for help."

The sorceress scowled. "I don't give help. Ever. To anyone."

She spun around with a swish of her robe. As she walked away, she grumbled, "Leave my lair now! Before I turn you both into worms and cast you into the marsh."

Vonya's eyes widened in fear that all her hopes would be dashed. "Wait! We came here for a different reason—to wager."

The hag stopped walking. Slowly, she turned around. "Wager?"

Vonya nodded, clinking her wagon wheel earrings.

Cackling with delight, Domnu cracked her withered knuckles. "Oh, I can never resist a good wager! What are the stakes?"

"If I win," replied Vonya, "you must bargain with me. Honestly, with no tricks. And if you win—"

"Then I will decide," finished the sorceress, "whether

to bargain with you . . . or to eat you alive." Malevolently, she grinned. "Not very high stakes."

Knowing she had no choice but to accept the terms, Vonya whispered to Shim, "Trust me, this is the only way."

He peered at her with equal portions of love and fear. "If you're sure . . ."

"I am."

"Good," declared Domnu. "What objects shall we use? Bones, perhaps? Or dice?" Waving toward the bowl of eyeballs, she added, "Or maybe . . ."

"Bones," declared Vonya with finality.

The old hag shrugged, disappointed not to have the chance to play with her eyeballs. "As you wish, my pet."

She snapped her fingers. Instantly, a ceramic vase appeared, floating in the air before them. Five thin bones protruded from the top of the vase, their tops poking equally high above the rim.

Pointing at the bones, Domnu said, "One of them is taller than the rest. Whoever chooses that bone wins the wager."

She waited a moment, then added, "Think carefully, now. Here are your choices."

Casually, she flicked a finger at each bone, one at a

time. As she did so, an invisible bell rang out, sounding a different note for each bone.

While Vonya's attention stayed entirely on the bones, Shim kept his eyes on the sorceress. Her face remained totally impassive as each of the bells sounded—until the very last one. For that bone, the bell sounded the lowest note of all . . . and when she heard it, Domnu grinned ever so slightly.

What does that mean? wondered Shim. *Is she cheating?*

Before he could voice his concern, Vonya reached for a bone. She picked one from the middle of the vase and pulled it out. Because it was as long as the vase itself, it seemed like a good choice.

Immediately, Domnu reached over. She chose the bone for which the lowest note had sounded. As she drew it out, it kept on coming and coming, stretching impossibly—until it finally came free, fully three times as long as the vase. Seeing this, Vonya shuddered and released a mournful howl.

"Too bad, my pet," clucked the sorceress in satisfaction. "You lost our little wager."

"Wait now—" Shim started to object. But Domnu interrupted him.

"As a consolation, though . . . I won't eat you. Instead, we will bargain." More to herself than to them, she added, "A good bargain is almost as much fun as a wager."

Vonya heaved a sigh of relief.

Suddenly, Domnu frowned. "Too bad you don't have anything valuable to bargain with. I have enough giant bones and teeth already. And you don't have any jewelry . . . except for those ugly earrings, and I have no need for wagon wheels. Maybe we should just go back to the plan of eating you alive."

"I do have one thing," insisted Vonya. "And it could be very useful to you."

Domnu gave the giant a skeptical stare. "What is that?"

Drawing herself up to her full height, Vonya answered, "My life."

Shim waved his arms in protest. "No, no! You can't!"

She shot him a determined look. "Remember your promise," she said firmly. "Now stay quiet."

"But—but—"

"Quiet!"

Shim ground his teeth, then reluctantly nodded.

"Good lad," said Vonya more softly. Turning back to

the sorceress, she explained, "I offer you my life, to do whatever labors you require . . . for the rest of my days."

Domnu grinned wickedly, showing her crooked teeth. "That could possibly be useful."

The two of them locked gazes, each taking the measure of the other. From the chessboard came a piteous sound, as the unicorn whinnied in warning.

Finally, the sorceress spoke again. "I could use a servant, my pet. You are right about that." She gestured at the cavernous space around them. "Constant upkeep and repairs, this old lair requires that. And you are big enough to do the worst jobs."

Holding her gaze, Vonya declared, "I would do that. But only if you agree to my side of the bargain."

Practically bursting, Shim shook his head wildly. "No, no, no! This is truly terribibulous!"

Vonya raised her hand to silence him. "Your promise!"

Shim groaned like a wounded beast. "But—"

"Hush now. The sorceress and I have some bargaining to do."

Grudgingly, he obeyed. He looked down, grinding an enormous foot into the stone floor, but didn't say another word.

"Now then," said Domnu with a gleam in her eye. "What service could I provide you in exchange?"

Vonya sucked in her breath. "You could transform my son. Make him smaller. So he will never again be in danger because he's a giant."

Shim froze and practically fell over. The same bolt of pain he'd felt from the Living Mist struck him full force, squeezing his lungs and paralyzing his limbs. All he could do was croak weakly, "No . . . please, not that."

Mustering all her willpower, Vonya didn't look at her son. She kept her focus entirely on Domnu. "Well?" she asked the sorceress. "What do you say?"

"Hmmm . . . you want me to smallify him? So no one would ever suspect that he's a giant?"

"That's right."

"That is difficult magic, my pet. Very difficult. It would be much easier just to turn him into a worm or a flea. Are you sure you want him smallified?"

"I am sure." Her giant voice echoed around the lair.

Out of the corner of her eye, Vonya glanced at Shim. He was groaning in pain, barely able to move. The sight broke her heart—but not her resolve. If this was the only way to save his life, then she mustn't waver.

"So," she asked the sorceress, "will you do it?"

Domnu gazed at her without blinking. At last, she replied, "We have a bargain. But only if you will agree to one last wrinkle."

Suspicious, Vonya raised an eyebrow. "Which is?"

"When I smallify him, so nobody will ever suspect his true origins . . . I will also erase a little bit of his memory."

"That he was once a full-size giant?"

"No, my pet. He can certainly remember that—and all the rest of his former life. Except for one little piece—a rather unimportant detail."

"And that is?" pressed Vonya.

"You." Domnu stared hard at her. "He cannot remember his mother. Or most of what happened to him here in my lair. If he remembered that, he might come back here someday and try to rescue you."

Hearing those words, Shim gasped as the pains grew even more intense. Despite that, he looked pleadingly at his mother and tried with all his might to say something to stop her from this folly. His lips moved. But the only sounds he could make were raspy groans.

Vonya swallowed hard, blinking back her tears. She

nodded at Domnu. "All I want is for him to survive. So . . . yes. We have a bargain."

"Good. Let's not waste any more time." Lowering her voice, the sorceress noted, "You have a lot of work to do."

Vonya turned to Shim and pulled him close, wrapping him in one last embrace. Fighting back a sob, she whispered, "Just remember this, my jelly roll. Bigness means more than—"

She never finished. A flash of light exploded in the lair, so bright that for a moment she couldn't see. In the very same instant, her beloved son shrank down in size—so fast that she lost hold of him completely.

Shim, meanwhile, fell through her arms and slammed onto the floor. Dazed, he sat up. Though his head was spinning, he tried to focus. But everything around him looked terribly distorted. He shook his head, utterly disoriented.

Suddenly, in a flood of panic, he realized what had happened. His nose, his feet, and his hands were all still there—but they were much, much smaller, along with every other part of his body. Even his clothes had shrunken down in size.

"Smallsy!" he wailed, his voice sounding much higher

than he remembered. "I am smallsy and shrunkelled!"

He stood, looking everywhere for something—anything—that seemed normal. But none of his surroundings looked even remotely normal.

He stood only as high as the ankle of the giant who now towered over him. Staring up at her, he wondered who she was . . . even as he felt a sharp pang down inside himself, a feeling of emptiness that he'd never felt before.

Just then, Domnu—now much taller than Shim—strode over to him. With a menacing cackle, she bustled him over to the tunnel entrance and gave him a violent kick in the backside. He shrieked, tumbling all the way out into the Haunted Marsh.

With a snap of her fingers, Domnu slammed shut the tunnel's heavy wooden door. Under her breath, she growled, "That's the end of you, little giant."

"No!" shouted Vonya, blinking as her sight returned. "You sent him out there to die!"

"Not at all," countered the sorceress. "I sent him out there to live." With a toothy grin, she added, "As long as he can."

Vonya swung her fist angrily at the sorceress. But

with a mere flick of her finger, Domnu froze the giant's arm in midswing, as if it had been pinned to the very air. Though Vonya fumed and tried to move her arm, she remained completely stuck, unable to break free of the spell.

Scowling, Domnu glared back at her. "I kept my side of the bargain. Now you keep yours."

Crestfallen, Vonya relented. Sadly, she moaned, "I never even got to tell him goodbye."

Domnu flicked her finger again, releasing the giant's arm. "That wasn't part of our bargain, my pet. Now—get to work."

13.

EMPTINESS

S him gagged, struggling to get some air. Facedown
in a puddle of muck, with rancid ooze dripping into
his ears and clogging his nose and mouth, he forced
himself to move. *Breathe! I need to breathe!*

With a painful effort, he rolled over and sat up.
Dazed and aching all over, he coughed, sneezed, and
coughed again, expelling most of the muck. Then he
gave his head a furious shake, which sprayed fetid
liquid all around him.

Where exactly was he? As he wiped the gooey filth
off his eyes, he remembered only the merest flashes of

recent events—all of which seemed either impossible or too horrible to think about.

A hairless hag whose name he didn't know. A frozen unicorn. A sudden flash of light. A giant, someone he didn't recognize . . . and a feeling of great emptiness down inside. And in his ears, a strange voice saying, *Bigness means more than* . . .

Than what? he wondered, still feeling that pang of emptiness.

Then came other memories, even more horrible: He was falling—shrinking! Like that face in the mist . . . only this was really happening. To him! To the giant once called Big Feet. The same person who had proudly boasted, *Someday . . . I'll be the bigliest giant in history, higher than the highliest tree.*

He gulped, realizing the truth. Some of those memories were actually real. At least a few of them. But which ones were real, and which were illusions? Exactly how he'd been so cruelly shrunken, he couldn't recall . . . but he felt sure it had happened somewhere nearby. Or was that, too, just an illusion? So much of his memory seemed to be shrouded by an impenetrable veil.

Shim scanned the desolate, dimly lit scene. Swamp,

shadows, and more shadows. Behind him rose a rickety old building made of rocks that looked ready to collapse. Before him lay the most dreaded landscape in Fincayra. The Haunted Marsh.

But that wasn't nearly the worst of his troubles.

"No!" he cried, waving his tiny hands in front of his face. "I am not bigly, not bigly at all!"

Bigness means more than . . .

The words echoed in his mind, carrying no meaning but plenty of pain.

He shook his head again, trying to regain his composure. Like his own thoughts, the landscape before him held only darkness and shadowy beasts. The swamp's gloom felt heavy, broken only by the distant glow of wavering lights, the bubbling pools and poisonous fumes, and the occasional skeleton of a dead tree.

"Must go," he said aloud, as if speaking to an invisible companion by his side. Yes—he must go somewhere. Anywhere but here!

Groaning miserably, he pushed himself to his feet. He drew a deep breath, still remembering what it felt like to have an enormous chest and giant-size lungs—so very different from how he felt now.

Bravely, he faced the gloom. Then he stepped forward—and suddenly fell into a bubbling pit!

Muck swallowed him, covering his head, filling his mouth. At the same time, something seized him by the waist and tightened like a noose. It dragged him down, deeper and deeper into the pit.

In his last instant of consciousness, Shim knew that he had drowned.

14.

PRISONER

A huge yellow eye!

Seeing that eye, right next to his face, Shim tried to leap backward—but he was tightly bound, wrapped in coils of vines and tied to something immovable. But even more astonishing than the eye and his predicament was one simple fact.

"Alive!" he exclaimed. "I'm still alive!"

Slowly, the yellow eye blinked. The vertical slit of its pupil narrowed down to a thin, dark line. Then the head that held the eye pulled away, revealing the identity of Shim's captor.

"Ugh!" Shim cried in fright. He tried to wriggle away, though that made the vines tighten even more around his chest. "A snakely beast!"

"Ssssso you did sssssurvive, I sssssee." The creature with yellow eyes examined him, just as a vulture would regard a piece of carrion. "Welcome to the den of Sssssslaylo, king of the sssssswamp ssssserpentssss."

Trembling with fear, Shim peered at the huge serpent facing him. Behind the immense, triangular head stretched an incredibly long body that disappeared into the shadows of the muddy den. In the dim light from above, the serpent's scales gleamed the reddish color of rusted iron.

"Ssssssuch a very long way I carried you," said Slaylo, bobbing his head. "Down my ssssssecret tunnelsssss all the way to my den, never cccccertain that you were sssssstill alive."

Stretching out his long, forked tongue, the serpent caressed one of Shim's bare feet. As Shim tried to pull back, fighting against his bonds, Slaylo hissed with amusement. "Yessssss, you will be an exquisssssssitely tasssssty treat. Worth all my trouble to sssssssave you, clean you up sssssso niccccccely, and bind you."

The eye slits narrowed. "Essssspecially becaussssse I prefer to eat my treatsssss alive."

Shim tried again to break free to no avail. *This would never have happened*, he told himself angrily, *if I was still as big as a giant!*

Desperately, he scanned his surroundings to see if there was anything he could possibly use to escape. But all he saw, besides the massive serpent, was a den that reeked of snakeskin and stuffy air. Plus a pile of brush and dead leaves that filled one corner.

Looking up, he discovered that the dim light of the den came down through the trunk of a dead tree that reached up to the swamp. The tree's hollow column rose directly above them. Several of its roots dangled down into the den.

So, he realized, *I must be tied to one of those tree roots.* At once, an idea burst into his mind. If he could somehow free himself, maybe he could climb up one of the roots and escape through the tree? Of course, that would only get him back to the swamp . . . but at least he'd avoid becoming the serpent's next meal. Yet that plan was totally worthless with his captor so nearby. He needed to convince the serpent to leave him unguarded—but how?

"O splendid snakely king," he intoned. "It is a great honor to be sacrificed to your hunger."

Slaylo raised his head, clearly not used to being addressed with such respect by his prey. "I am sssssso glad you undersssssstand."

"I do, O great slimy and slithery one." He waited for the serpent to nod in approval, then continued. "But alas, there is a seriously serious problem! I am so very smallsy—and you, curly king, have such a huge appetite."

Slaylo's tongue slid hungrily over his jaw.

"So, your slitherousness . . . don't you want to get some more food to fill your long and lengthy stomach? I will wait here patiently for your return . . . knowing that my smallsy sacrifice will help to ease your great hunger."

Slaylo slid closer to study his unusual captive. "What ssssssort of creature are you, sssssmall one?"

"A giant," declared Shim, feeling a sudden surge of pride. Then, more sheepishly, he added, "Just . . . a very *little* giant."

Hissing laughter echoed around the den as the serpent shook with mirth. "You are cccccertainly no giant! You are the leassssst giant-like being I have ever sssssseen!"

Shim scowled, humiliated.

"Sssssstill," declared the serpent in a more serious tone, "you are right about ssssssomething. I am very, very hungry! And your ssssssmall ssssssacrificccccce won't be nearly enough."

Brightening, Shim suggested, "Tell me more about your hunger, O curlymost king."

Flicking the tip of his tail, Slaylo parted the pile of brush, revealing a large, green-spotted egg. "All the food I have besssssidesssss you isssss thissssss one egg . . . which I hope might ssssssomeday hatch. That way I can ssssssswallow alive whatever treat it holdsssss."

Shim couldn't help but cringe. How awful to be born just in time to get swallowed by this monster!

"Surely, great king, you should have more to eat."

The vertical sits of Slaylo's eyes narrowed again. "True. Sssssso I will leave you briefly to find ssssssome more food. Then, when I return, I will ssssssavor a sssss-sumptuousssss feassssssst."

"Good idea, your slitherousness! I shall wait for you to come back and swallow me royalishly."

Hissing with anticipation, the serpent replied, "Ssssso you shall."

With that, Slaylo turned and slid into the darkness, his undulating form moving swiftly across the mud.

As soon as the serpent's tail vanished from sight, Shim sprang into action. Sucking in his breath to loosen his bonds even a tiny amount, he jostled himself lower and lower—hoping that the tree root would narrow toward the bottom. Hard labor though this was, he gave it all his strength. For he knew that his life—even as small as it was now—depended on it.

Gradually, he moved lower on the root. But the vines still held him tight. *Harder!* he urged himself. *I must . . . try . . . harder!*

Vines chafed against his ribs, his arms and legs, even his neck. He panted hoarsely from exertion. Yet with every muscle in his body, he continued to wriggle downward.

At last—he felt a sudden loosening of his bonds. He'd reached the lowest point of the tree root. Seconds later, he pulled himself out of his bonds, casting the vines aside.

Free! He was free!

He started to climb up the dangling root, hoping fervently he could escape through the hollow tree before the serpent returned. Just as he pulled himself off the den floor, however, he stopped. For he realized there was something else he needed to do before he left this dreadful place.

Shim dropped back to the floor and dashed over to the brush pile. Carefully, he lifted the green-spotted egg. Although it was as big as his own head, it felt surprisingly light, and he stuffed it into his shirt. After making sure the shirt's bottom was securely tucked into his leggings, he scurried back to the root. And with all the speed he could muster, he started to climb again.

Just then, he heard an ominous sound—a heavy body sliding across mud. From somewhere in the distance came a harsh hiss.

Slaylo! Coming back so soon!

Upward he climbed, pulling himself from the root into the trunk that rose high above the den. Bit by bit, he edged higher . . . ever mindful of the egg he carried. One arm and leg at a time, he rose closer to the open hole at the top of the dead tree.

Below him, the hissing grew steadily louder. Suddenly, it rose to a shrill, earsplitting shriek.

"Ssssstop! Sssssstop now, you are my prisssssoner!"

Shim worked his way higher. The hole above him, where dim light filtered down into the den, drew nearer and nearer and—

Snap! Deadly jaws closed just below him, barely missing his foot. Shim glanced down to see the serpent's yellow eyes, seething with rage. The jaws opened again, impossibly wide, ready to bite off his legs.

Suddenly, a loud screech filled the air. Before he knew what was happening, powerful talons grabbed Shim by the shoulders and yanked him upward—just as the snake's jaws slammed shut, catching only air.

Astonished, Shim flew out of the hole and across the open swamp. Compared to the stuffy air of the den, the marshlands' fog seemed like a fresh breeze from the mountains. Looking up, he saw the immense body of a greathawk, one of the biggest birds on Fincayra. But while he could have held the bird in one hand when he was a full-size giant, now the greathawk carried him with ease. The bird's massive wings pumped steadily, carrying him far away from the vicious serpent.

In a heartbeat, Shim's relief at being rescued turned to dread. Had he been saved just in time to be eaten by somebody else?

15.

WINGS

The greathawk flew over the fog-shrouded marsh-lands, clasping Shim in her talons. Then she veered sharply, raising the angle of her powerful wings. A sudden *whhooosh*—and she hovered, hanging motionless in midair.

Surprised, Shim looked down to see an enormous tree right below them. Though it, too, was dead, this tree was much more massive than the one above the serpent's den.

"That bigly tree!" he exclaimed. "It's truly a gi—" But the word caught in his throat.

Like a great wooden temple, the tree lifted its arms skyward. Grand even in death, it stood majestically, with deep ridges running through its ancient bark. And in the center of its crown, it held a vast nest of interwoven branches.

With a piercing screech, the greathawk released Shim. He landed in the nest, much more gently than he'd expected, cushioned by the thick layer of feathers that lined its inner bowl. As he sat amidst the feathers near one side, the bird landed on the rim just above him.

Ruffling her wings, the hawk peered at Shim with round, golden eyes. Shim stared back, trying his best to look more confident than he actually felt. Had he just moved from one predator's dining room to another?

"Welcome, fledgling." The greathawk's deep voice sounded like a faraway horn in the forest. "I am glad," she said, "you will live another day."

"You're not going to eat me, then?"

Before hearing her reply, Shim tried to stand. But he lost his balance in the mass of feathers and tumbled over backward. By the time he'd righted himself and sat down again, he saw that the bird was still watching him . . . but now with a look of amusement in her eyes.

"No, fledgling, I'm not going to eat you. I am Rowallon, guardian of this nest. And who are you?"

"Shim," he replied. "I am a giant! Even though . . . I don't really look like one."

Rowallon clucked merrily. "If you're a giant, then I'm a thundercloud. Except that I'm not." Leaning closer from her perch on the rim, she asked, "Now tell me the truth. What kind of creature are you, really?"

Flustered, Shim shouted, "A giant! Just like I said."

The greathawk merely stared at him.

Shim hung his head. "I'm just . . . a little giant. The littlest one everly."

Kindly, she reached out a wing and brushed his shoulder. "Whatever you really are, you were nearly devoured by Slaylo."

"Yes, but you saved me just in time." His expression full of gratitude, he said, "Thank you so very muchly, Rowallon."

"I was glad to do it." Sadly, she shook her head, making the small gray feathers on her face tremble. "I only wish . . ."

"Wish what?"

She sighed. "I only wish I could have saved someone

else from that serpent. Someone I loved dearly."

Compassionately, Shim whispered, "Who?"

Rowallon clacked her beak and made a mournful sound. "My child. Just yesterday, while I was taking my morning flight across the marsh . . . he struck. Climbed up to this very nest, he did—and stole my first and only child."

She fluffed her wings, as if trying to sweep away the sadness. For the first time, Shim noticed the richly varied colors of her feathers. Gray, brown, and white feathers formed wavy bands across her wings and tail. And the feathers on her chest, while mostly gray, showed flecks of radiant green.

All at once, Shim understood. Carefully, he reached inside his shirt and pulled out the green-spotted egg. Undamaged, it rested snugly in his hands. Offering the egg to the greathawk, he said, "Methinks this might belong to you."

She screeched in utter surprise. Leaping into the air, she stretched out her talons, took the egg, and flew several joyful circles around the tree. At last, she lowered the egg into the downy feathers in the middle of the nest and gently sat on top to keep it warm.

Quietly, she cooed, "You are safe now, little one."

With a new light in her golden eyes, she peered at Shim. "You may not look like a giant . . . but you can still do giant-size things."

Bashfully, he waved away her compliment. "Really, I'm just a regular, ordinarious, run-of-the-mill—"

She clacked her beak, cutting him off. "You're like nobody else, Shim."

"I know," he said sadly. "Like nobody else."

"That isn't a bad thing," she insisted, opening her wings to their widest. "Listen to me now. You see this majestic tree we're in?"

"Sure. It's hard not to see something so . . . bigly."

"This tree," she explained, "is the kind humans call a lodgepole pine. That's because when these trees grow close together in the forest, they look nearly identical. They all grow straight and narrow—very tall, but also very much alike."

Shim crinkled his nose in puzzlement. "But this one is so massively massive, not narrow at all."

"Exactly." The greathawk puffed out her chest feathers, covered with vibrant green flecks. "Only when a lodgepole pine stands alone, completely free, as this one did for centuries, can it grow to its full size—and its unique self."

Slowly, Shim nodded, weighing the meaning of her words. Once again, from a distant part of his memory, he heard the words, *Bigness means more than . . .*

He couldn't remember the rest of the sentence, or even who had spoken the words. And he still wasn't sure what they really meant. But he did feel sure they'd been said with affection, maybe even with faith in him . . . just like the words of the greathawk.

He reached over and touched the tip of her wing. "I'm so glad you and your child are back togetherly now."

"So am I," said Rowallon with an emphatic clack of her beak. "I can feel the life, the heartbeat, inside the shell. And I know we will have many wonderful times together."

She cocked her head thoughtfully. "You may not fully understand this. But I am the mother of this little one— and a mother will do anything, anything at all, for her child."

Something about her words, or maybe her attitude, seemed vaguely familiar to Shim. He wasn't sure how, or why . . . but he felt moved in ways he couldn't describe. Happy and sad at the same time.

"Now," said Rowallon, "is there anything at all I can do for you?"

Shim's eyes gleamed. "There is one thing. A most helpfulous thing."

16.

A VOICE

After carrying him across the Haunted Marsh, Rowallon gently lowered Shim onto a grassy knoll. Standing there, he could see, stretching far into the distance, the dark fog of the swamp—just as he could still hear the wailing of ghouls and smell the odor of decay. But Shim knew now that this place held more than just danger and death.

It also held a friend.

Feeling the soft green grass under his feet, he gazed up at the huge bird hovering over him. Her powerful wings beat the air, while she flexed the talon that had so easily carried him. In her other talon, held securely, was a beautiful egg with green spots on its shell . . . for she had vowed never again to leave it unguarded.

Looking straight into the greathawk's golden eyes, Shim said, "Thank you so muchly much, Rowallon."

She screeched and replied in her deep, resonant voice, "And thank *you* so muchly much."

She wheeled in midair, then called out, "Come back someday to meet my child. Until then, fledgling, travel with care!"

With a *whhooosh* of her wings, she departed. Shim watched her as she flew away, holding the gleaming egg. Soon she vanished into the rising mists of the marsh.

Turning away, the little giant surveyed his surroundings. On the side of the knoll away from the swamp, rolling green hills beckoned. Surely, amidst those groves of oak and spruce and aspen, there would be some good food to eat. Maybe nothing as tasty as those ubermushrooms he'd eaten on his last night in Varigal . . . but good nonetheless.

Those mushrooms were his last clear memory before everything got terribly vague and hard to recall. It felt as if a thick veil had fallen across his mind, obscuring much of what had happened. Though he couldn't

remember how, he knew that he'd fled the horrible attack of Stangmar's warriors . . . and somehow ended up
in the Haunted Marsh.

How did he get all that distance from Varigal, all by
himself? That was a real mystery . . . though not as great
a mystery as how he'd been shrunken down so cruelly.

As his stomach growled, his thoughts returned to
food. One food in particular—honey. Just the idea of his
most cherished treat made his mouth water.

He started to stride down the knoll—but abruptly
stopped. For some reason, he turned around to look one
last time at the Haunted Marsh. Why? He didn't understand. He simply knew that something about that place
called to him . . . tugged on him . . . awakened a strange
yearning inside him.

He shrugged—and turned away. Probably he was
just feeling pangs of hunger. How long had it been since
he'd eaten? Too long, for sure.

"Honey!" he exclaimed, smacking his lips. He
needed to find some, like he'd done so many times before. Suddenly remembering his much smaller size, he
reminded himself, "But nowadays I need to avoid any
buzzers so I won't get stingded."

Down the grassy slope he tramped, surprised at how much slower he covered ground than he recalled doing until very recently. Whatever strange thing had happened to him, making his legs so much smaller, his appetite seemed just as big as ever.

"Honey," he repeated as he waded across a tumbling brook at the base of the knoll. Cold water splashed him, soaking his leggings and chilling him to the bone. Longingly, he recalled the days when he could have stepped over this brook with a single stride—days he'd never know again. He shivered . . . and not just from the cold.

And so Shim's wanderings began. Hours turned into days, days into weeks, as he roamed aimlessly across the hills, forests, and plains of Fincayra.

Over and over again, whenever he encountered others, he tried to explain that he was really a giant. The response was always the same—total disbelief, usually accompanied by laughter and derision. It happened when he spoke to the girl who was milking her cinnamon-colored cow, the family of monkeys who taunted him from their home in a banyan tree, the stern centaur who galloped off in disgust, and the ancient healer who paused making her poultice to hear his tale of woe . . .

and then promptly offered him an herbal remedy to stop hallucinations.

And many more times besides. Even a colony of sparrows, who had heard him lamenting out loud, tumbled out of their nests and rolled on the grass in uncontrollable laughter.

Making matters worse, he was starting to doubt himself. "Was I ever really a giant?" he grumbled as he climbed up a rocky hillside. "Or was that all just a wild, hallucinatalous dream?"

Topping the hill, he caught the unmistakable scent of honey on the breeze. He froze, sniffing so avidly that his nose trembled. Somewhere down in the ravine below him, he felt sure, was a tree full of honey. The familiar urge to gorge on honey, biting into the sticky combs and drinking all the liquid sweetness he could hold, rose up inside him.

Yet . . . something felt strangely different. The old urge vanished as quickly as it had appeared, leaving him mystified.

He scratched his head, trying to understand. But for some reason, he didn't really feel in the mood for honey right now—something that had never happened before. Not once, in his entire life.

"Maybily," he muttered, "it's because my back is so sore and covered with welts from getting stingded so badly yesterday? Or maybily . . ."

He paused, almost afraid to say the words. "Or maybily loving honey was just another wild dream?"

A raindrop struck the tip of his nose. Then another, and another. Within seconds, clouds darkened overhead and thunder boomed across the hillside. A downpour began.

Shim ran down the hill, hoping to find some shelter from the storm. Spying a stream whose rocky banks held several overhanging slabs, he veered in that direction. Rain pounded down, soaking him and making the ground slippery, but he managed to find a protected hollow beneath a slab. He dived inside and rolled to a stop.

Immediately, he smelled the remains of a partly eaten fish. As well as musky, wet fur. Looking behind him, he discovered a young otter who had stopped chewing on a trout to stare at him.

"Who are you?" asked the otter, resuming his task of devouring the fish in his paws. "You don't look like anyone I've seen before."

Shim ran a hand through his wet, scraggly hair.

Glumly, he said, "That's because there's nobodily else anywhere like me."

"How nice," bubbled the otter. Having finished his meal, he tossed the fish bones aside and started to lick his whiskers. "In my family, everyone looks like everyone else, and like all the other otters in the world. And we all like the same games, too. Not much variety . . . though we do have fun playing together."

Shim replied sadly, "At leastly you know who you are and where you come from."

The otter started, his whiskers trembling in surprise. "You don't know that? Honestly?"

"Honestly."

Widening his dark brown eyes, the otter said, "That's impossible."

"No, it's not." Shaking his head, Shim explained, "Once I was a giant—a bigly, strong giant. Or at least . . . I think that was true. Now, though, I don't know what in the worldly world I am."

The otter stared for a moment, then suddenly clapped his paws together. "Ha! You almost fooled me there! For a second, I thought you might be telling the truth. But you're really just joking, aren't you?"

Shim hung his head.

"Well," the otter said cheerily, "I've got to go now. Off to meet my friends at the big slide downstream." As he rushed past Shim, he added, "Nice hearing your jokes!"

Rolling his eyes, Shim muttered, "They're not my jokes. They're . . . my life."

Looking beyond the overhang, he saw that the thunderstorm had stopped. Outside, sunlight sparkled on the rain-washed stones and reeds. The stream clattered past thousands of colorful pebbles that lined its borders—blue turquoise, red iron, yellow sulfur, and black obsidian, all shining in the sun.

Yet none of that was enough to cheer him up. Frowning, he clambered out to the stream, which spilled over one edge to form a crystal-clear pool. As he knelt by the pool to take a drink, he noticed a waterfall just upstream that he hadn't seen before. Though narrow, it flowed strongly, crashing downward. After the rainstorm, so much water poured down that the waterfall looked like a rippling white curtain.

Shim turned back to the pool, which was lined with many of the bright blue pebbles. Cupping his hands to get water, he grumbled, "Back in oldentimes, I could have swallowed this whole pool in one bigly gulp! But now . . . *nobodily* believes me that I was once a giant."

He sighed morosely. "Even I don't believe me."

Suddenly, from the far side of the pool, came a faint ringing of bells. And a tiny whispering voice that floated up to his ears.

"I believe you."

17.

THE LEAPER

Astonished, Shim dropped his hands and stared at the pool of water. Among the sunlit blue pebbles on its rim, one shone brighter than all the rest. With a gentle ringing sound, it flew into the air and hovered right in front of his face. Like a tiny blue star, it glowed with its own shimmering light.

"Elf!" cried Shim. "It's you!"

The luminous faery looked deep into his eyes. "Yes, it is," she answered with a joyful shake of the bells on her antennae.

"You look even more lovelyish than before."

"And you," she replied, "look much, much *smaller* than before. Whatever happened to you?"

Shim groaned. "I really don't know! All I remember is the attack by Stangmar's gobsken, a reeky and bleaky swamp, and then—somehow, I got utterly shrunkelled."

Elf gazed at him, puzzled. With a whir of her translucent wings, she quickly flew a circle around him. As she came back around to face him, she shook her golden bells regretfully. "You certainly were, as you say, shrunkelled!"

His slim shoulders sagged.

"But," she added more brightly, "I will still call you Big Friend. After all, you're still a whole lot bigger than me!"

For the first time in weeks, Shim laughed out loud. Elf joined him, ringing her antennae bells as she hovered.

At last, Shim's mirth calmed enough that he could speak.

"When we said goodbye before, you told me, *Go now . . . and live with light.*"

"Right. But what does that have to do with you getting shrunkelled?"

"Well," he replied with a hint of a grin, "maybily I

thought you said, *Go now and get very light*. And so I did!"

Both of them laughed again.

Finally, Shim gave her a grateful look. "It's been too longish since I got all chuckly like that. About anything."

"Me too." Her blue glow swelled. "I'm glad to see you again."

She swooped closer and landed on his left shoulder, weighing no more than a windblown seed. "Let's go look at that waterfall," she suggested. "I like how it pours down into the stream."

"So do I. Waterfalls make me feel all peacefully inside."

Shim strode over to the white veil of water, carrying the faery on his shoulder. He sat down on a stone right next to the falls.

After a while, Elf spoke again. "I remember the last thing you said, back when we met before. You declared, *Certainly, definitely, absolutely!*"

His brow furrowed. "I don't say that anymore."

"Why not?"

"Because it sounds . . . too giantly. It just doesn't feel right anymore."

She rang a somber note. "I'm sorry this happened to you, Big Friend."

Compassionately, he replied, "And I'm sorry that evilous wyvern happened to you."

Her luminous form dimmed, making her wings seem more gray than blue. "We both know what it's like to lose our family, our people."

Something about her words made Shim feel again that pang, that emptiness—as if part of himself had been cruelly ripped away, stolen forever. Whatever peacefulness he'd felt from sitting next to the waterfall had now vanished.

Elf shuddered, making her bells chime discordantly. "On that day the wyvern attacked, I also lost something else."

"What?"

"A magical crystal. One of the great Treasures of Fincayra. It's been guarded by my people for centuries."

"The famously Treasures," said Shim, suddenly recalling the dismal visions of Lunahlia from that last night in Varigal. "Our evilous king is searching for them, right? Nobody knows why. I heard he's already taken several of them, like the Flowering Harp."

Elf's faery light dimmed even further, leaving only the faintest blue glow along the edges of her wings. "After you left, I searched all around our destroyed cavern for the crystal. But it had disappeared."

"Wait!" exclaimed her companion. "Was it all orange and shiny-like?"

"Yes!" Much of the faery's radiance returned. "You saw it?"

Shim nodded grimly. "That evilous wyvern took it. I saw him grab it in his claws."

The color of Elf's body darkened to steely blue. "That wyvern, I found out after the attack, is called Gasher. He loves to terrorize any creatures smaller than himself— which means basically everybody else. Except, of course, a gi—"

She caught herself before finishing the word. But Shim knew what she'd meant to say.

"A giant," he said glumly. "Go on."

"Well, Gasher had never attacked a faery colony before that day. Which is why he caught us by surprise. Killed everyone but me. And stole our precious crystal."

She shuddered, making her bells sound like breaking glass. "All this makes frightful sense—I see that now.

Gasher serves Stangmar, who must have promised him great rewards for doing the king's dirty work."

"Including stealing Treasures."

"Right," wailed the faery. "I can't imagine what terrible things Stangmar could do with the crystal's enormous power!"

"What exactishly," asked Shim, "is that power?"

"Leaping instantly to another place," she answered. "That's why we call it the Leaper. Its power lets you move in a heartbeat to any other place, no matter how far away."

"In a heartbeat," repeated Shim, awestruck.

"One more thing," continued Elf. "Legends say the Leaper can only be used by someone whose heart is true and whose motives are right."

"Then what could the wickedly king possibly do with it?"

The faery chimed some somber notes. "The legends also say that the crystal could possibly be corrupted, turning its power to death and destruction. If it ever fell into the wrong hands . . . it could be changed into a weapon that's able to cast foes—even whole armies—to their deaths."

Enraged, Shim vowed, "We can't let that happen!"

"True. If the king could change the Leaper into a weapon like that, he and Gawr could wipe out anyone who dares to oppose them."

Standing up, Shim turned toward the waterfall. Swiftly, much faster than he'd expected, he felt calmed by its beauty and grace. He gazed thoughtfully at the cascade of water—a lovely liquid curtain, endlessly flowing. Mist from the falls caressed his face; splashing and swishing filled his ears.

Quietly, he spoke—as much to himself as to his friend. "Despite all our troubles, there is still so much beauty in our world. Beauty that needs saving . . . and helping . . . and loving."

Turning to the faery on his shoulder, he added, "Which is why we are going to get back your crystal."

"We?"

"Yes indeedily! What do you say to that?"

She glowed bright from the tips of her wings down to her toes. "I say thank you, Big Friend!"

She scrutinized him, still not sure she could believe her ears. "You would really do that? You would make us a team?"

"A truly intrepidly team."

Her light dimmed. "But we have a serious problem."

"I know," he said anxiously. "How are we ever going to defeat such a terribibulous foe? Even when I was all bigly and strong, that wyvern was almost too much for me."

"That's a problem, for sure. But before we even get to that one . . . we have another."

Shim cocked his head. "What?"

"We don't have even the slightest clue where Gasher might be. Or whether he still has the crystal—though most likely he kept it for a while, just to possess it. But even if he still has it, we probably won't have much time left before he delivers it to Stangmar!" She shook her bells despondently. "This is a very big island, with hundreds of places for wyverns to hide. So we have no idea at all where to look."

Both of them abruptly froze. Something was emerging from the waterfall!

Slowly, from a spot in the cascade above Shim's head, it pushed out of the falls. Delicate and glistening, it stretched outward, reaching toward them.

A hand.

18.

SECRET HIDEAWAY

The hand, looking almost as liquid as the waterfall itself, reached out from the flowing curtain. Shim and the luminous faery on his shoulder both watched, entranced, as the watery fingers stretched toward them.

"Somelyhow," said Shim, "I don't feel afraid as much as . . ."

"Amazed," finished Elf. "Just amazed."

The hand, now fully protruding from the waterfall, abruptly stopped. Then, as water flowed around its wrist, the hand beckoned to the companions.

"It wants us to come closer," said the faery, sounding her warning chimes.

"No. Methinks it wants us to come . . . inside."

They traded uncertain glances, then Shim stepped forward. Covering Elf with his hand to keep her from getting washed away, they entered the tumbling cascade. Water crashed down on top of them as they moved through the falls.

And then, all at once, they entered a wondrous chamber, unlike anything they'd ever known.

They stood inside the falls, directly behind the torrent of water. Mist, shot through with rainbows, swept around them ceaselessly. Strange translucent plants, part liquid and part solid, sprouted from the walls and dangled from the ceiling like fruity dewdrops—some resembling cherries, apples, and pears, while others were simply liquid leaves that dripped constantly. One wall held a row of slender, pointy vegetables, hanging like icicles that sparkled with silver-colored frost. Nearby grew rich green moss that seemed to flow down a face of rock, next to a bubbling, translucent tree that resembled a slow-motion fountain.

"Thank you for joining me, brave travelers."

Shim and Elf turned to see a woman with deep blue-green eyes and silver braids that flowed like sunlit streams down to her waist. Wearing a rippling, sea-green gown and an amulet made from an iridescent shell, she radiated elegance. Gracefully, she bent to sit on a stone so that she could face her guests directly rather than look down on them.

Gesturing around the chamber, she asked, "Do you like my watery home?"

Elf waved her antennae, making them chime sweetly.

"Oh yes," answered Shim. "It's so wetly wonderful in here."

She grinned. Then, speaking rhythmically with the cadence of ocean waves, she explained, "I made this secret hideaway many years ago, when I sensed the first little rivulets of trouble forming . . . in case they should ever swell into raging rivers. Rivers that could drown our beloved isle of Fincayra."

Shim tilted his head, trying to understand. "You mean trouble from King Stangmar?"

The woman fingered the spiral shape of her amulet. "Yes."

"You know him, then?"

"Yes," she answered somberly. She stared off into the distance for a moment. "You see . . . he is my son."

Shim almost fell over backward into the curtain of falls. "Then you are . . ."

"Olwen." She bowed her head in greeting. "I imagine you have heard a few stories."

"Only one, and it's a beautiful one," replied Elf, shaking the moisture off her wings. "About your love for our wizardking Tuatha—a love so great that you left your ancestral home under the sea to join him."

Olwen nodded. "That is true. I also gave up my graceful merwoman's tail, trading it for these." She patted her legs. "And I would do that again a hundred times, so deep was our love for each other." She sighed. "I just never expected that our time together would end so soon."

Shim grimaced. "So it's true, then? Tuatha defeated that wickedly Gawr and banished him to the spirit realm, but died in the process. How horribobulous!"

"That's the right word for it. And now my son has taken the throne." Her voice roughened like waves crashing on a rocky shore. "But he is merely a tool for Gawr, who manipulates him from the spirit realm."

She turned her blue-green eyes up to the ceiling,

recalling some painful memories. "The first command that came from Gawr was to kill me, since I represent a threat to Stangmar's rule. So I was forced to escape, running for my life from the new king—my own son."

She faced them again, her eyes as misty as the air of the hideaway. "At least, before I left, I helped his wife, Elen, escape with their young son, my grandson—a boy they call Emrys . . . though I suspect he will someday earn a true name, one befitting a wizard. If, that is, he survives! Unlike Stangmar, the boy has the gift of drawing magic from nature. So he, too, threatens the king's power . . . and Gawr's control."

She paused, biting her lip. "I only hope the Living Mist and the ocean beyond will be kind to them. Elen's plan is to journey all the way to the world of mortals, her homeland, where Stangmar can never find them. Perhaps my kin, the merfolk, will guide them to safety. That's possible, since the boy has some of my mer blood in him. But there is no way to know."

Lifting her amulet, she placed the shell against her ear, listening. She held it there for a long moment, her expression wistful. Whether she was just hoping to hear its familiar sound of the sea, or perhaps even a word of encouragement, the companions couldn't tell. But they stayed silent until she finally lowered the shell.

"Even now," Olwen continued, "the king's army of gobsken and ghoulliants are slaving night and day to transform an ancient temple into his fortress, a castle that will forever spin on its foundation. It will be dreadful—and impossible to attack."

She shook her head. "It pains me to see that old temple destroyed. Long ago, it was built over a sacred spring and dedicated to Lorilanda. You already know, I'm sure, that she is the great goddess of birth, flowering, and renewal—as well as the partner of Dagda. But you might not know that Lorilanda is especially revered by my people, because so much of the life of this world resides in water—the oceans, the rivers, the lakes, the streams. So it was natural to build her temple over a spring with its own special magic. In fact, there is no place on Fincayra with more power . . . outside of Druma Wood and the Crystal Cave of Elusa. Which is why Gawr wanted to put the new castle there at the spring—to tap into that magic and divert it to evil."

She scowled. "Bad as that is, Gawr has ordered Stangmar to do something even worse—to send his most vicious warriors to destroy the giants! It doesn't even matter to Gawr or my son that the giants are Fincayra's oldest people, a race that deserves to be honored, not hunted. All because of some prophecy called—"

"The Dance of the Giants," completed Shim. With a shudder, he said, "I know this to be truly."

"How?"

He drew a deep breath and stood his tallest. "Because, Lady Olwen, I am a giant! Not a giantly giant, I know— just a little giant. But, believe me, I really am one."

She listened, watching him closely. And most strikingly, she did not laugh.

With a jostle of bells, Elf spoke up. "Stangmar has also sent his warriors and allies to hunt for the Treasures of Fincayra."

Olwen peered at the faery with compassion. "Like the Leaper."

Elf bobbed her antennae. "But why?"

"Because the Treasures, including the crystal guarded for so long by your people, hold enormous power. And Gawr wants to turn that power to evil purposes, corrupting all the Treasures into weapons."

"That's why," declared the luminous faery, "we must

find the Leaper before it's too late." Her glow dimmed. "The trouble is . . . we have no idea where to look for Gasher, the purple wyvern who stole it."

Olwen gazed at her guests for several seconds, fingering her amulet. At last, she announced, "I do."

Both Shim and Elf caught their breath.

"As a child," Olwen explained, "I played along the southern coast of the isle, in the shallows near the fabled Shore of the Speaking Shells." She tapped her amulet. "Where I found this old friend."

Leaning closer to the companions, she went on. "One day, in the cliffs just west of that place, I discovered a nest of wyverns. Purple wyverns."

Elf radiated blue light. "That's where Gasher must be! Oh, thank you for helping us!"

"Yes," agreed Shim. "You are a greatly friend."

She locked gazes with him. "And you, I am certain, are much more than you seem. I can see the giant in you, even now."

Shim puffed out his chest. "Thank you muchly, great Lady."

Olwen's oceanic eyes turned to the faery on his shoulder. "You, too, have a great heart, much bigger than your body. I am sure your family is very proud of you."

Elf's light dimmed like the moon hidden by clouds. "I lost my whole family when the Leaper was stolen."

Olwen looked at her with great compassion. "So you have no mother or father?"

The faery's wings sagged.

Her voice a mere whisper, Olwen said, "I can understand your loss, little one. For I am a mother who lost her only child. He may still be alive . . . but he's no longer my son."

No one spoke for some time, as the falls flowed, the liquid plants dripped, and the mist swept all around them.

Finally, Shim said quietly, "My father, somelybody told me, died fighting against Gawr. But I don't even remember my mother."

Olwen reached out her hand and gently stroked his cheek. "You once had a mother, you did. She is with you even now—in ways you may not fully understand."

She smiled lovingly. "And I am certain that she would see the giant you truly are."

Again Shim felt the sudden surge of longing— and the painful emptiness that came with it. A voice he couldn't quite recognize whispered in his memory something about the true meaning of bigness. But who had said that to him? And why?

As Olwen withdrew her hand, the little giant continued to look at her. "Maybily someday your son will remember the wonderful mother who is still inside *him*."

"That," she replied, "is the kindest thing anyone has said to me in a very long time."

Shifting her gaze to the luminous faery, Olwen declared, "May Lorilanda strengthen you, little one. For centuries, your people have guarded the Leaper and kept it safe. Now it needs your protection, more than ever."

Elf chimed resolutely. "That is my quest. The crystal can't become a weapon for Gawr!"

"Right," agreed Olwen. "What will happen to the other Treasures of Fincayra remains a mystery. But the fate of this one, the Leaper, is up to you."

"And me," declared Shim. "It's my quest, as well."

On his shoulder, Elf brightened.

But Olwen shook her head. Studying Shim, she said, "The Leaper is only part of your true quest. Maybe even the smaller part. Trust me—I feel sure of that."

Confused, he peered back at her. "Saving the Leaper

will be perilously enough! If that's not my only quest, then what else do I need to do?"

She drew a deep breath of the misty air. "That's for you to discover."

"I just hope I'll survive that longishly."

"So do I," replied Olwen.

"And so do I," echoed Elf.

Straightening her back, Olwen looked at them with a mix of hope and fear . . . as well as admiration. "Go now, brave travelers. But you must hurry! If that wyvern hasn't already given the Leaper to Stangmar and Gawr, he will soon!"

Shim and Elf nodded with grim resolve.

"Here is something to give you strength on your journey." Olwen reached up and plucked a pear-shaped fruit from a vine. As she offered it to her guests, it shimmered and sparkled like a watery crystal. "My aquapears have just ripened."

Shim received the fruit with both hands as the faery floated down to it. Elf took the first bite, then Shim followed. Nectar ran down both of their chins as they swallowed their first morsels of the luscious, sweet flesh. Eyes open wide with delight, they kept eating, taking many more bites, until the aquapear had been reduced to just a tiny stem and a few seeds.

"Fank woo muchwee much," said Shim through a mouthful of fruit.

Elf glowed and rang her golden bells melodiously.

Watching them eat, Olwen smiled. As they finished, her smile faded away. "Farewell, brave ones. Great danger awaits you . . . and great hope for Fincayra goes with you."

19.

BEWARE

Fueled by Olwen's exquisite fruit, the companions left her waterfall hideaway and set off immediately. Shim strode as fast as his little legs allowed, while Elf chose to ride on his shoulder, her glowing wings pressed close against her back. Over the rolling hills they trekked, always aiming southwest, toward the Shore of the Speaking Shells.

After several hours, they reached the edge of the mighty River Unceasing. Crossing it proved far more difficult for Shim than last time, both because the river had widened greatly toward its delta and because he couldn't just step right across as he'd done before. Only after another hour of searching did they find a bridge of river stones close enough together that Shim could hop from one to the next. But the stones didn't reach all the way to the other side, so Elf took flight and Shim dived from the last stone into the swiftly flowing water. Madly, he swam to the opposite shore. Though the current carried him a good ways downstream, he finally pulled himself onto the bank, soaked and bedraggled.

"Swimming is for fishes and merpeoples, not for me!" He shook his wild mane, spraying Elf, who was hovering right above him.

"You made it, though." With a sarcastic jingle of bells, she added, "No danger of you ever becoming a merman."

"No, surely not." He felt the urge to say, *Certainly, definitely, absolutely*—but resisted. Those words belonged to his past.

Before long, they started walking again. Soon the landscape to the west grew more verdant with shrubs and grasses that vibrated with life. Colorful birds soared overhead, weasels and foxes prowled, butterflies darted and crickets sang, while young deer leaped gracefully over pools and stones. A long-billed curlew whistled mellifluously from the grasses. In the distance, the greenery deepened even more, melting into a swath of enormous trees that reached majestically skyward.

Perched on her friend's shoulder, Elf's light strengthened. "Over there is the Druma Wood, the most magical place in all of Fincayra."

Shim stopped, turning toward the forest. His nose quivered, sensing diverse smells that ranged from damp mushrooms to an ancient badger's den. And more kinds of trees than he'd ever known. He smelled the sweet resins of hemlock and spruce, the cinnamon of moss oak, the meatiness of walnut, the rich vanilla of elmgrace, and plenty of mysterious scents he couldn't identify.

"Magical for surely," he said in a reverent tone.

"They say that forest holds even more mysteries than it holds creatures. Birds who fly upside down. Lizards who sing like nightingales. Bubble beings who can change the future. Why, there's even one tree that grows a different kind of fruit on every branch!"

Elf's antennae rang enthusiastically. "Only the woodswoman Rhia, who lives deep in the forest, knows all its creatures. And the stories say she speaks with every one of them, in their own languages. She lives inside a huge oak tree called Arbassa."

"Rhia. A nicely name. What else do you know about her?"

"Not much. Except that she wears a suit of woven vines that stay forever green."

Glumly, Shim ran a hand through his hair, still sopping wet from crossing the river. "I'm sure I'll never meet her—it's too unlikely. A great famously person like her and a forgettable little . . . whatever I am."

The faery leaped off his shoulder and hovered directly in front of his face. Angrily, she declared, "The only time you're forgettable is when you talk like that! Don't you remember what Olwen said? *I can see the giant in you, even now.*"

"I guess so." He frowned. "It's just hard to feel that way sometimes, now that I'm so smallsy."

Elf landed on the tip of his nose. Looking at him with affection, she said gently, "Your body may be smaller now, but you're still the same brave hero who fought off that wyvern. I'm sure of that."

Listening, he stood a tiny bit taller.

"And besides," she added mischievously, "compared to me, you are still an enormous giant."

He couldn't help but grin. Glancing again at Druma Wood, he said, "Somedaily I'd really like to come back and explore that place. And maybily," he added with a wink at the faery, "meet that woodsywoman, Rhia."

Elf leaped up and hovered by his ear, so close that he could feel the gentle wind from her whirring wings. "The best way to explore a new place . . . is with a friend."

Shim bit his lower lip thoughtfully. "We both lost our families, Elf. But we do have this—our friendlyship."

"That we do." The faery hovered closer, reached out her tiny hand, and touched the edge of his ear. "Want to know how I define *friends*?"

"Sure."

"Well," she explained, "friends are the family we choose for ourselves."

Shim nodded.

With a graceful swoop, she returned to his shoulder. But at the same time, her luminous wings dimmed. "I only wish . . ."

"Wish what?"

"That at least my sister had survived. We were identical twins—exactly alike, right down to our golden bells."

Her antennae drooped. "She and I were the only ones

in our whole colony to have bells this color. So we could recognize each other across even a big meadow or lake."

Shim reached up and, with the tip of his finger, gently touched her wingtip. "You still have somelybody who is your family."

Her bells chimed harmoniously.

Seeing a grassy knoll that rose nearby, Shim jogged up to the top, carrying Elf on his shoulder. From that spot, the vista stretched far indeed. To the north, they could see the gleaming ribbon of the River Unceasing. Very far in the distance, a thin column of mist shot through with rainbows rose into the sky. Might that be, they both wondered, mist rising from the waterfall that held Olwen's secret hideaway?

Looking west, they viewed the vast expanse of Druma Wood, shining with more shades of green than Shim had ever dreamed possible. Huge trees lifted skyward, every one of them even more majestic than the pine that bore the nest of the greathawk Rowallon. Like immense pillars that supported the sky, those trees towered above the forest floor, sheltering thousands of wondrous creatures in their branches, under their bark, and among their roots. Brightly feathered birds swooped and soared above the highest canopy of leaves.

Somewhere out there, Shim knew, stood the grand oak tree that Elf had said was the home of the woodswoman he hoped someday to meet. As well as the wondrous tree that grew many kinds of fruit. And out there, as well, lived all those magical creatures she had named—and so many, many more. Creatures most people had never seen . . . and who lived nowhere else in the universe.

Filled with awe, he blew a long breath. "Fincayra really is an amazingly place! Full of so much magic and mystery."

Turning to the luminous being perched on his shoulder, he declared, "We surely do live in a special place, Elf."

She met his gaze. "Which is why we must do everything we possibly can to save it."

"Starting with getting back the Leaper! Before that ghastlyish Gasher hands it over to the king."

With a discordant jingle, she added, "If he hasn't already."

"Let's go! Next stop—the oceanly coast and that place we heard about from Olwen."

"The Shore of the Speaking Shells."

Immediately, Shim started down the knoll with the faery riding on her perch. Through much of the day, they marched southward, crossing through wide grasslands, serrated ridges, and windblown groves.

At last, Shim caught the briny smell of seawater. Ocean birds circled overhead, screeching and cawing and clacking their beaks as they flew. The ground grew more sandy, the grass more sparse. They topped a row of dunes—and suddenly found themselves facing a wide, rocky shore.

Tide pools, full of spiky sea urchins and tiny blue and yellow fish, dotted the coast. Colorful shells lay everywhere, often draped with glistening fronds of kelp. Shards of driftwood bobbed in the shallows, while waves lapped endlessly on the shore.

Out past the waves hung a dark, vaporous wall. The Living Mist. For a moment, Shim peered at it, understanding at last the mist's terrible warning at the Giants' Cliffs. *I wish,* he thought, *the mist had a different prediction for me now.*

But the mist didn't reveal anything. It merely hung there—heavy, dark, and foreboding.

Finally, Shim turned away, walking to the west among

the tide pools. So he never saw the Living Mist gather itself into the shape of a powerful winged beast slashing with its deadly claws. Lightning flashed within the mist, and the shape abruptly shifted to a hairless hag with unblinking eyes . . . a giant laboring to lift a massive stone . . . and a strange island in the middle of a lake.

Soon, beside the cries of seabirds and the ceaseless sighing of the waves, the companions heard another sort of sound. All around them, the shore seemed to be whispering, as if the very sand was breathing. Or perhaps . . . talking.

"Shells," they both said at once, realizing what was the source of the sound.

Shim bent to pick one up, a green shell that rested by a tide pool. Round and polished by waves, it fit nicely in the palm of his hand. Gleaming with a rich luster, its curves were edged by fine red lines. Slowly, he raised the shell and brought it up to his ear. Elf leaped into the air and hovered close by.

To their amazement, the shell spoke with slow, whispery words. Words that were clearly meant for them.

"Bewaaaaare, *splashhh*, you must bewaaaaare."

"We will try," answered Shim. "But can you tell us

how to succeed? We need to find a wickedly wyvern and take back a stolen treasure . . . without dying miserously."

The shell blew a long, uncertain breath. "No one, *splashhh*, can tell you that. *Splishhh sploshhh.* Not even Washamballa, sage among the shells, knows the answer. So you must, *splashhh*, bewaaaaare. Bewaaaaare!"

Grimly, Shim returned the shell to the tide pool. Elf fluttered back to his shoulder. Together, they continued down the coast, eyeing the stark cliffs that rose on the horizon.

All the while, whispery voices surrounded them, ceaselessly saying the same sinister word.

20.

A PLAN

As the companions drew closer to the cliffs, the ground grew more rocky and steep. Soon they left behind the Shore of the Speaking Shells, though they could still hear, in their memories, the green shell's whispered warning.

Waterbirds continued to circle overhead, screeching and whistling, but they were different kinds than they'd seen and heard among the tide pools. These were mostly terns, puffins, and red-legged kittiwakes who nested in the cliffs. And while the continuous sigh of waves still accompanied them, keeping almost the same rhythm as Shim's breathing, the shoreline grew more distant as they climbed higher.

With the cliffs looming before them, Elf paced anxiously on Shim's shoulder. "I hope you have a plan for how we're going to do this."

Shim groaned. "I was hoping *you* had a plan."

Together, they studied the steep ridge ahead of them. Made of dark, volcanic rock, the cliffs formed a vertical wall facing the sea—far too treacherous to scale. Sharp pinnacles jutted skyward like daggers of stone. Even if someone could successfully climb that wall, it wasn't possible to predict where the wyverns' nest might be hidden. Only by viewing the cliffs from a distance—from somewhere out in the shallows—could anyone tell. Which is how, long ago, Olwen had discovered the wyverns' location.

"How do we even find that greedyish thief, let alone take back the crystal?" wondered Shim.

The faery's blue light flickered unsteadily. "I have no idea. It's impossible to see the nest except from the sea . . . or—"

She caught herself. "I have an idea! You keep walking up this slope that will take you around to the back side of the cliffs. I'll meet you up there at the top."

Before Shim could say a word, she lifted off and buzzed toward the cliffs.

Watching her tiny blue glow depart, he realized what her plan must be. *Except from the sea . . . or the air.* He swallowed, willing her to be careful. She was the very last of her kind. As well as his friend.

He began to plod up the slope. As he gained altitude, the slope grew increasingly dangerous. Sharp rocks poked out of the ground, deep pits gaped, and crevasses cut across the landscape. All these obstacles slowed his progress—and made him wish again that he still had the long legs of a true giant.

Yet he kept going, climbing the slope bit by bit. Once, when he leaped across a crevasse, he landed on a loose rock that broke off under his foot. He fell forward, safely on the other side, his heart pounding as he listened to the rock clatter down into the fissure below.

Suddenly, he heard a terrifying shriek. A wyvern! The fierce beast, with wide purple wings, soared directly above him. Shim stayed utterly motionless, hoping the wyvern wouldn't notice him among the rocks.

He held his breath as the wyvern passed overhead.

Daring at last to look up, he saw no sign of the missing scales on one wing that would identify the beast as Gasher.

I wonder, he worried, *how many more wyverns we're going to find in the nest.* Would Gasher be among them? And would he recognize Shim, even in his much-reduced size, from their battle?

As he watched, the wyvern veered toward the cliffs and then plunged downward, disappearing somewhere among the dark pinnacles.

Slowly, the little giant regained his feet. Then all at once—he froze, sensing something new.

His nose trembled. Amidst the briny smells of the ocean, which included kelp and crabs, fish and seawater, he detected a different scent.

Smoke.

Maybe, he reasoned, those wyverns kept a fire in their cavern, something to cook whatever they ate. And if they had that, maybe they also had a way for the smoke to escape—some sort of chimney.

He continued climbing up the slope. Careful to avoid the rims of crevasses or pits, he moved steadily higher— following his hunch as well as the trail of smoke.

Finally, he reached the top. To one side, the slope ended abruptly in the impassable cliffs that faced the ocean and the swirling mist beyond. To the other side, the ground angled down much more gradually toward the lands he'd recently traversed. Cautiously, he approached the upper edge of the cliffs.

He halted. Rising out of a pit near the edge was a thin, curling plume of smoke.

A familiar buzzing sound caught his attention. He whirled around to see Elf zipping swiftly toward him.

She landed on his shoulder and spread her luminous wings. "I found it!" she exclaimed. "It's a cavern, down below us in the cliffs."

Hurriedly, she continued. "It's filled with purple wyverns—at least six of them. And the leader, bigger than all the rest, is Gasher."

"Is he missing a bunch of scales on one wing?"

"Yes," she cried excitedly. "But there's another way I know it's him—the beautiful orange crystal he's guarding!"

"Good. Then we're not too late."

All of a sudden, her excitement faded and she shook her bells glumly. "Trouble is, there's no way for you to get to the cavern. Those cliffs are impossible to climb. And there's no other way for you to get there."

"Well," answered Shim, "maybily there is."

"What do you mean?"

"Tell me, did those wyverns also have a cooking fire?"

Elf started. "Why, yes. They were roasting some poor creature they'd just caught."

Shim walked over to the pit, with Elf floating beside him. When she saw the thin plume of smoke, she protested, "You're not thinking of climbing down *that*, are you?"

"Sometimes," he replied, "I is full of madness." His brow furrowed, for there was something very familiar about those words. Who had said that to him recently?

Pushing that question aside, he pointed at the pit. "The wyverns use this tunnel for smoke to get *out*. So they'd positivitously never expect anyone to use it to get *in*."

"But," protested the faery, "it's full of smoke! How could you possibly breathe?"

Peering down into the pit, Shim shook his head. "It's smokily, for sure. But I also smells fresh air coming up, smelling like wyverns and roasting meat and old bones."

Something about those words pricked his memory. Wasn't there someplace he'd been recently that had a lot of old bones? He shrugged, sure that it wasn't anything important.

Elf rustled her wings nervously. "Even if you can somehow climb down to the wyverns' nest and survive . . . what happens next?"

Shim rubbed his chin, thinking. Finally, he declared, "If I can make it all the way down there—"

"Without dying from smoke," interrupted Elf worriedly.

"If I can just get there—"

"And not fall into their cooking fire," she interrupted again.

Giving her a stern look, he tried once more to explain his plan. "If I can just get there, you can fly down the cliffs and meet me. Then . . . maybily you can cause some sort of distraction. Get those wyverns all focused on killing you."

"Mmm," she mused sarcastically, "I love this plan more and more."

"And then, while you're distracting them, I can grab the crystal."

"Then what?"

"Then," he answered decisively, "we use its power to leap! Somewhere very far away." Lowering his voice, he asked, "Errr . . . you *do* know how to use it, don't you?"

"No!" she cried, jangling her bells. "All I know is that the Leaper can only be used by someone whose heart is true and whose motives are right."

Shim exhaled slowly. "Well, then . . . we'll just have to figure out that part when we get there."

"*If* we get there."

He gazed at her with determination. "This is our bestly hope."

She shook herself nervously, then finally agreed. "All right, Big Friend."

21.

DOWNWARD

Shim turned toward the ocean and gazed at the dark wall of mist beyond the shallows. The Living Mist revealed no hint of his future . . . except, perhaps, for its oppressive darkness.

He clenched his jaw. Would his plan, such as it was, lead him to the wyverns' nest? To the magical crystal? And even if he succeeded in getting there, would he then be torn to shreds by Gasher?

Elf leaped off his shoulder and hovered beside him. Watching him anxiously, she sounded a shaky chord with her bells.

Shim took a deep breath. Bending down, he tore a strip of barkcloth from his leggings and tied it over his mouth like a kerchief. Then he faced the pit.

Mindful of the unstable rocks on the rim, he slowly lowered himself into the hole. Immediately, smoke poured over him. With all his concentration, he sought any fresh air that also flowed up the tunnel. Finally, he found a thin stream of better air.

Breathing slowly, he started to descend. Finding footholds wasn't easy, especially in the smoky air that stung his eyes and obscured his vision. But he managed to feel his way downward, using his toes to locate small outcroppings that he hoped would support his weight.

Sometimes, as he descended, the tunnel filled with a belch of smoke so thick he had to hold his breath and shut his eyes until it passed. Other times, fresh air swept over him, allowing him to breathe more freely and see clearly. In those moments, he climbed down as fast as he could.

At one point, the tunnel veered sharply to the side so it became almost horizontal. Shim crawled through that section as swiftly as possible, scraping his arms on the jagged walls. Soon, the tunnel turned and dropped straight down again.

Suddenly, he reached a place where the tunnel narrowed. The walls pinched closer and closer, squeezing him on all sides. He grimaced, trying to work his way lower. But progress was painfully slow.

Ugh, he thought, *I never thought I'd wish to be more smallsy!*

Just then another thick cloud of smoke passed over him—making it impossible to breathe. All he could do was hold his breath until it passed. But what if it lasted too long?

He stifled a cough, knowing that any sounds would echo down into the wyverns' cavern. When he couldn't hold his breath an instant longer, he drew a sharp breath—but it was all smoke. He coughed loudly, unable to help himself, again and again.

Finally, the thick cloud passed. Cleaner air filled the tunnel—as well as his lungs. With great effort, though his throat felt raw, he made himself stop coughing.

Taking advantage of the burst of good air, Shim squeezed himself lower. The walls scraped him brutally. But he moved gradually downward, slowly edging nearer to the nest of wyverns.

Just as he placed his foot on a nub of rock—it broke

off! Suddenly, he slid downward, out of control, unable to stop. Desperately, he thrust out his arms, his legs, and also his head—anything that might arrest his fall.

At last, he slowed himself enough to grab hold of a narrow lip of stone. He hung there, panting. Though he'd stopped falling, he ached all over, sporting bloody scrapes on all his limbs as well as his neck and shoulders.

A loud shriek erupted from below. The cry of an angry wyvern!

Had he been discovered? Had that falling rock alerted the wyverns to his approach, so that they were waiting to devour him as soon as he reached their cavern?

For several seconds, he waited. How, he wondered, was this going to end?

Hearing no more angry cries, he continued to climb downward. After a while, the tunnel began to widen slightly. He started to hear new sounds from below—snarls and growls, but no more shrieks.

The first hint of light drifted up into the tunnel. Meanwhile, he heard the scraping of claws on stone and the crackling of fire. He smelled, apart from smoke, meat roasting and a hint of sea breeze. Yet the most powerful smell overwhelmed everything else, and couldn't be mistaken.

Wyverns.

Carefully, he drew closer to the end of the tunnel. Though it had widened considerably from the narrowest section, it remained snug enough for him to brace his body as he descended. The light grew steadily stronger, as did the smells and sounds.

At last—he reached the bottom of the hole. Painstakingly bracing himself against a rock that protruded from the lower rim, he peered down into the space below.

Purple wyverns filled the cavern. Two were wrestling on the floor, another pair were comparing the size of their jagged wings, and one lay sleeping by the wall. Near the entrance was an enormous pile of shiny objects—gold coins, silver goblets, and all sorts of precious jewels. At the top of the pile, in a place of honor, sat an orange crystal that glowed from the reflection of the fire . . . as well as its own inner light. The Leaper.

Shim clenched his jaw angrily as he looked at the sixth wyvern, the largest of the group, who sat next to the pile. Gasher looked as smug as he could be, enjoying the glint of the crystal, despite his many battle scars.

Among the worst of those, Shim noted with satisfaction, were the jagged scar on the wyvern's jaw and the missing scales on one of his wings.

Directly below Shim, the remains of an ox sizzled on a huge spit. Just beneath the carcass, a roaring fire blazed, its smoke curling up toward the tunnel.

Suddenly, Shim spied a quick flash of light on the cavern wall. Blue light! After the flash died away, he saw a tiny little form crouching there on a ledge.

There you are, brave Elf.

The friends' eyes met. Across the cavern, they watched each other, poised to leap into action. Both of them knew that this was their only chance to take back the precious crystal and keep its great power from being turned into a weapon by Stangmar or Gawr. And both of them also knew that their chances of success were exceedingly small. How could they possibly prevail?

Shim's thoughts, though, had turned to a more immediate question. How was he ever going to get down from this perch . . . without getting smashed or burned to a crisp?

At that instant, the rim rock supporting his weight broke loose.

22.

TRUE OF HEART

As the rock broke off, Shim tumbled downward, plummeting into the wyverns' cavern. Straight toward the blazing fire below!

Even as he plunged, limbs flailing and hair blowing, a split-second memory flashed across his mind: the last time he'd fallen. But that fall was very different—through the arms of someone enormous, someone mysterious. And that fall wasn't into a blazing fire.

Instantly, he snapped back to the present—just in time to smash into the ox carcass roasting over the flames. *Crash!* He slammed into the ox, snapping the wooden spit and causing an explosion of flaming coals, burning ox meat, and sizzling sparks.

He bounced off the carcass and flew through the flames so fast that he avoided getting roasted; only his hair and leggings were singed. With a thud, he landed on his back on the cavern's stone floor, shaken but still alive. As he sat up, the entire cavern burst into chaos.

Gasher, along with the rest of the wyverns, shrieked in surprise. Countless hot coals and sparks rained down on them. Havoc erupted.

The wyvern who'd been fast asleep woke abruptly when a big shard of burning wood from the spit landed right on his snout. Screeching in pain, he whipped around—and struck another wyvern in the face with the heavy ball of bone at the end of his tail. That wyvern, thoroughly enraged, roared in fury and pounced on her attacker, shredding part of his wing with her massive claws. As they wrestled viciously, those two wyverns rolled into another one—causing him to shriek and attack them both ferociously.

While all this was happening, Elf watched from her ledge. She knew that her only hope to help Shim get the crystal was to buy him some more time. And the best way to accomplish that was to add to the chaos. Which was why she decided that instant to do the bravest thing she—or any luminous faery—had ever done.

She leaped into the air. Like a glowing blue missile, she flew directly at Gasher's face. With every bit of strength she could muster, she hurled herself right into one of his wide purple eyes.

"Aaaarrrghh!" roared the dragon-like beast in agony. Rearing back, he clawed at his face to remove whatever had struck him.

Elf, meanwhile, dropped to the cavern floor. Stunned by the impact, she lay there unconscious, her radiance almost gone. She was helpless to prevent one of the wyverns from stepping on her or rolling over her, which would surely crush her to death.

Unaware of Elf's sacrifice, Shim regained his feet. As fast as his little legs could scurry, he ran to the wyverns' pile of treasures. He jumped onto the glittering mass of goblets, nuggets, jewels, belts, daggers, crowns, amulets, bracelets, and coins. Swiftly, he climbed to the top—and grabbed the most precious treasure of all.

The Leaper.

The crystal's orange glow, magnified by all the flames

around the cavern, made it seem like it was itself on fire. But it felt as cold as a river stone in Shim's hands.

Anxiously, he glanced over at Gasher. The enormous purple wyvern, who was angrily clawing at his face for some reason, hadn't yet noticed him. Nor had any of the other wyverns, too busy screeching, slamming, and slashing at each other to pay any heed to an intruder.

Where is Elf? he wondered, scanning the cavern. But he saw no sign of her. All he could do was hope she was unharmed—and would soon join him.

He hefted the crystal. To his former self, it would have been smaller than one of his fingernails. Now, though, it completely filled one hand. Just to be safe, he held it with both of his cupped hands. How was he supposed to make it work its famous magic? Could he actually get it to carry him and Elf to safety before their time ran out?

Peering at the Leaper's glowing facets, which shimmered with light, Shim couldn't shake the feeling that it was somehow alive. Like a crystalline eye, it seemed to be watching him. Observing him closely, inside and out. Deciding, perhaps, whether he was truly worthy of its help.

What had Elf told him about its power? That it could

move people instantly, taking them far away in just a heartbeat. Glancing again at Gasher, who had stopped clawing at his eye and seemed to be rapidly regaining his composure, Shim thought anxiously, *A few heartbeats is all the time I have.*

His mind raced. What else had she said? That the Leaper could only be used by a certain kind of person, someone whose heart was true and whose motives were right.

Well, he knew for certain that his motives were right—to get him and Elf out of here, and very far away, before they were totally destroyed by wyverns! So that left only one question: Was his heart really true?

Shim gulped. Fears flooded his mind. Just as he wasn't big anymore, he probably also wasn't brave or good or worthy. Maybe, back when he'd been a great and powerful giant, he'd possessed an equally great heart— one that was loyal and honest, caring and true. But that wasn't remotely possible now, in his shrunken little form. Why, he was really as far from having a true heart as he was from being a true giant!

Even so . . . he needed to try. His hands shook with concentration as he whispered, "Leaper! Get us out of here! Send Elf and me somewhere else. Right now. Before it's too lately!"

Nothing happened.

"Please, great crystal. Get us out of here!"

Nothing.

Anxiously, Shim looked again at Gasher, who was doing his best to stop the other wyverns from killing each other. He roared wildly, jumped into the fray to separate combatants, and forcefully smacked one on the head with his massive tail ball. Seeing that wasn't enough to restore calm, he hurled another wyvern into the wall, hard enough to rock the entire cavern.

Shim knew that, as focused as Gasher was now on subduing the others, it wouldn't last long. Soon the wrathful beast would turn his attention back to the pile of treasures—and to the intruder who was trying to steal the most valuable one of all.

Just then, Shim heard a familiar whirring of wings. He spun around to see the faery flying toward him, a bit wobbly but clearly alive.

"Elf! Where in the worldly world have you been?"

"Oh, just helping out," she said blithely as she returned to her perch on his shoulder. Giving his neck a nudge with her wing, she teased, "Though when it came to causing a distraction, you didn't need much help from me."

In no mood for humor, he replied, "Well, I sure do now! I'm a failure with this crystal, Elf. Nothing I do is working!" He grimaced. "I'm just not . . . true of heart."

"You certainly are!" she objected, chiming her bells vigorously. "Come on now. Try again."

Squeezing the crystal with both hands, he said in a fervent whisper, "Please, Leaper. Help us escape! Now, while we still—"

Abruptly, he stopped, sensing something new at the edge of his vision. Turning, he saw it—and froze. Gasher was looking straight at him!

Having finally succeeded in restoring calm, the wyvern had swung around to face the pile of treasures. And discovered a robbery in process!

Gasher roared in rage, loud enough that several stalactites broke off the ceiling, plunging down like stone daggers. One of them impaled another wyvern in the neck, making him howl in pain. But Gasher took no notice. All his focus—and all his rage—remained squarely on the thief who had dared to enter his cavern.

Suddenly—Gasher ceased roaring. His gaze met Shim's. As the two pairs of eyes, one purple and one pink, stared at each other, the wyvern's expression changed. Though he still looked every bit as angry and vengeful as before, his face now showed something different.

Recognition.

Sure, Shim was much smaller in size than when they had met before. But with his bulbous nose, pink eyes, and wild hair, he still looked enough like the giant who had caused Gasher so much injury and humiliation that the wyvern recognized him. And hated him with every cell in his gargantuan body.

Gasher roared again, so loud that Shim's ears almost burst and Elf nearly fell off his shoulder.

Knowing they had no time to spare, Shim hastily turned back to the crystal. Though he couldn't hear his own voice over the wyvern's roars, he pleaded, "I know I'm not a bigly giant. But I promise you, my heart is true!"

Drawing a quick breath, he added, "And my motives are right, too. Just to save our lives! That's all I'm asking!"

From the corner of his eye, he could see Gasher raise

his deadly claws to attack. Then the wyvern leaped right at him!

Even as Gasher's immense body lifted into the air, flying toward him, Shim was seized by a new idea. Maybe his motives really *weren't* right, after all. Could they be just too small, too selfish?

He closed his eyes, concentrating. "Do this not just for me, not just for Elf. Do this, I beg you, for all of Fincayra! To save this whole beautifullous world! To keep your power from falling into the hands of the evilous king in his castle!"

He felt, on his neck, the hot breath of Gasher. And he knew for sure that time had finally run out. Yet . . . he also knew, in a way he couldn't describe, that he'd done his best.

In the last remaining instant before the wyvern's jaws closed on him, Shim suddenly heard voices. A surprising chorus of voices. They filled his mind, speaking with such clarity that they drowned out the wyvern's furious roars.

"You may not look like a giant," called the greathawk Rowallon from her tree, "but you can still do giant-size things."

"Yes," agreed the seer Lunahlia, swishing her long white hair. "Always remember that you really are a giant."

Olwen watched him with oceanic eyes. Then she said in her watery voice, "I can see the giant in you, even now."

"Your body may be smaller now," declared Elf with a shake of her bells. "But you're still the same brave hero."

Last of all came the voice of someone he could almost—but not quite—recall. And though he couldn't name the speaker, he heard, finally, all of her words: "Bigness means more than the size of your bones."

Just then, Gasher's teeth-studded jaws snapped closed—on thin air.

Shim, Elf, and the crystal had completely vanished.

23.

FORTRESS

Shim opened his eyes, utterly amazed to be alive.

Lying on his back in a grove of birch trees, he smelled the rich, loamy scent of forest soil. Still not sure he was really alive, he gazed up at the tracery of white-bark limbs and supple green leaves, with the late afternoon sky beyond. A gentle breeze stirred the leaves, making them whisper and swish.

Suddenly, he heard another sound—the familiar whirring of tiny wings. Right above his face appeared the faery he knew so well, her entire body pulsing with blue light. With a harmonious jingle of her antennae, she landed on his nose.

"You did it, Shim. You freed the magic of the Leaper!"

"Well, amazingishly . . . I guess that's so." He squinted, trying to focus on her while she stood on the tip of his nose. "And you did your part, too, my wingedly friend."

Elf laughed with a peal of bells. "All I did," she said modestly, "was give that miserable Gasher a headache,"

Squinting harder, Shim replied, "You're going to give *me* a headache, too, if you stay in that crossly-eyed place much longer."

"Happy to move," she answered cheerily. "But don't start bossing me around now. Just because you saved our lives, humiliated that wyvern, stole the crystal, and protected Fincayra."

"All in a day's work," he said with a grin.

"A *giant* day's work."

His grin widened.

As he sat up, still feeling surprised to be in one piece, Elf lifted off and settled herself on his shoulder. With a jolt, he realized that he didn't know what had happened to the Leaper. Had he lost it? Had it disappeared for good?

Relief swept through him like a powerful river as he saw where it rested. In his hand! He squeezed it, sending it a silent, simple message of gratitude.

Clasping the crystal, he slid it into the biggest pocket of his leggings. He noticed that his leggings' barkcloth material had been repaired several times, carefully stitched together by someone. Touched by that person's kindness, he wondered who could have done it.

A sharp pang of loneliness and loss struck him. *Who was that kindlyish person? And why can't I remember?*

He stood, planting his bare feet on the moist forest soil. All of a sudden—he stiffened. For there, in the vale, just below the hillside grove where they'd landed, was the very last thing he expected to see.

"The Shrouded Castle," he exclaimed. "Stangmar's new fortress!"

The faery's bells shuddered.

They stared, aghast, at the fortress. Almost finished, it bore imposing turrets and battlements, as well as dozens of murder holes for warriors to shoot arrows from or pour boiling oil on any unwanted visitors. Hundreds of gobsken warriors, muscles bulging under their sweaty green skin, labored to haul the remaining materials— heavy stones for walls, iron bars for windows, and hefty beams for archways.

Ghoulliants, meanwhile, floated around the castle's perimeter, shrieking commands and herding gobsken. Even from the distant hillside where they stood, Shim and Elf could see the hollow eyes and decomposing flesh of the ghoulliants' faces.

Shim moaned painfully. It felt like a living nightmare to encounter these warriors again, seeing them for the first time since their horribly brutal attack on Varigal. Some of these very same laborers, no doubt, had impaled his friends and neighbors with poisoned spears or sliced off giants' hands with broadswords.

The castle itself rose from the once-pristine vale like a monstrous scab. But in this case, that scab covered a uniquely deep wound—the destroyed temple of the goddess Lorilanda, the place Olwen had described so lovingly. All that remained of the temple's ancient spring, which had been sacred for millennia to Fincayrans, was a muddy spot by the castle wall. Where so many worshippers had knelt to drink from the spring or sing to its magic, there were now just the footprints of warriors.

"Already," said Elf grimly, "you can see horrible fumes starting to pour out of those windows. Fumes that will someday shroud this place completely."

"I can smell them, too." Shim crinkled his nose in disgust. "We're far enough away that I'm getting just a hint . . . but it's bad. Really bad. Like hundreds of thoroughly rottenous eggs."

Elf's wings darkened. "That's fitting, since Stangmar is also, to use your phrase, thoroughly rottenous."

Tapping the bulging pocket that held the crystal, Shim shook his head in bewilderment. "But why did the Leaper bring us here, of all places? Why not somewhere more lovelyish?"

The faery stamped her minuscule foot on his shoulder. "Because, you oaf, you named this place when you made your wish! Don't you remember? You said something about the evil king in his castle."

As if in agreement, the crystal flashed with light inside his pocket, making the barkcloth glow orange.

"Ugh," admitted Shim. "You're right."

"You'll have to be more careful next time."

"If," he replied, "there *is* a next time. That whole experience was pretty frightfulous."

Elf's radiance brightened. "But you did it! You saved us—and also kept the Leaper out of Stangmar's grasp.

That's what we faeries call *a mountainous miracle*."

"Thanks, but it took two of us to climb that mountain. Now we'd better get out of here before we're discovered by some of those scarily warriors. Besides," he added with a glance at the sky, "the sun is going to set pretty soon."

"Ready when you are, Big Friend."

He smiled, always glad when she called him that. He started to turn away from the castle, then caught himself.

"Before we leave, I just have to ask you something."

The faery walked across his shoulder and touched his earlobe. "Yes?"

"Do you really think it's possible that Stangmar could make that castle spin, as Olwen told us? It looks way too bigly to ever turn on its foundation."

"Hmmm. That depends on whether his master, Gawr, has succeeded in tapping the magic of the sacred spring. If he has . . . then plenty of wicked things are possible."

Shim nodded gravely. "Let's hope he hasn't. And let's also hope Olwen's wish comes true that the magical child, her grandson, really did escape from this place."

"Yes! Fortunately, Olwen did say that he went with

195

his mother . . . and as everyone knows, a mother will do anything to protect her child."

He didn't know why, but those words made him ache down inside.

Booooom!

A sound like a hundred thunderclaps exploded from the castle. The ground shook with violent tremors—so powerful that Shim almost fell over backward and Elf leaped into the air.

Seconds later, the soil around the castle erupted with huge crevasses. Those cracks radiated outward, snaking swiftly across the vale. One of them raced up the hillside where Shim stood, toppling several birch trees and cutting so close to him that he needed to leap aside to avoid falling into the crevasse.

Then, as the companions watched in astonishment, the castle began to turn. Creaking loudly as stone rubbed against stone, it started to spin.

Caught by surprise, many gobsken who were climbing ladders that rested against the castle's outside walls screamed in panic and fell to their deaths, crushed by loose stones that tumbled from the battlements. Others, even less lucky, fell into the gaps around the castle's foundation, where the turning stones ground them into bloody dust.

As the tremors finally ceased, the faery returned to her perch on Shim's shoulder. Though she didn't speak, her bells trembled with jittery, frightened notes.

24.

THE CHASE

For a breathless moment, the two companions watched Stangmar's castle spin slowly on its foundation. The hillside grove of birches where they stood no longer seemed the least bit tranquil. Instead of the gentle sound of wind-swished branches, the harsh, grating noise of stone grinding against stone rent the air.

Ominous signs touched all parts of the landscape. Any birds who hadn't already taken wing did so now, fleeing the vale as fast as possible. Boulders in the surrounding hills, shaken loose by the tremors, tumbled and slid, smashing into farmers' homes and wagons.

Meanwhile, to the west, the sun had started to set, painting everything dark red.

"We should leave swiftishly," declared Shim.

Elf's antennae chimed in agreement. She paced nervously on his shoulder.

Turning his back to the castle, Shim started to march, careful to avoid toppled trees and deep crevasses. At the crest of the hill, he strode rapidly through the last of the birches before descending into a gully that expanded into a ravine carved by centuries of melting snows in springtime. Reaching the bottom of the ravine, he turned to face—

Gobsken! A patrol of three muscular warriors, wearing their helmets and body armor, had just entered the opposite side of the ravine.

"Look there," called one gobsken, pointing his broadsword at Shim. "Intruder!"

"Or spy!" rasped another.

The third gobsken struck his shield with his sword. "Let's skewer him, mates."

The patrol charged at Shim, waving their swords wildly. At the same time, Shim spun around and hurtled down the ravine. Elf leaped into the air and, with a whir of wings, zipped ahead to seek out any possible way for them to escape.

Racing as fast as he could, Shim sped through the ravine, leaping over broken branches and rocks in his path. The gobsken barreled behind, cursing and shouting. Fortunately, their heavy, iron-wrought armor, as well as their broadswords and shields, slowed them down. Their boots slammed into the turf as they pursued their prey, neither gaining on him nor falling behind.

Shim veered into another ravine that merged with a wider watershed dotted with twisted fir trees laden with purple cones. Panting from exertion, he chanced a quick look behind, only to see the three gobsken also enter the watershed. They looked angrier than ever, huffing under the weight of all their armor and weapons but seething with rage.

"Stinking spy," rasped one as he brandished his sword.

"Die, you snake," called another hoarsely.

One of the gobsken shrieked as he caught his boot on a tree root, brutally twisting his ankle. He slammed to the ground with a spray of mud.

Still hotly pursued by the other two, Shim hoped desperately that he could outlast them. But his legs ached and his feet seemed to be turning into stone with every stride. "Can't ... do this ... muchly longer," he grumbled.

A thought struck him: Could he use the Leaper? Yet he knew there wasn't time—those gobsken would catch up and chop him into pieces before he could even take the crystal out of his pocket.

Trying to tire the gobsken further, he drew on every last morsel of strength and veered to climb a steep knoll. He leaned forward, finding a path between thornbushes and boulders, pushing himself higher. Hard as it was to keep going up the slope, he hoped maybe it would be even harder for those warriors. Even so, he needed all his concentration to keep from stumbling.

By the time he reached the top, he could barely lift his feet. His lungs screamed in pain. And he knew he was so exhausted that he'd soon drop.

He looked back—and saw the two remaining pursuers pounding up the slope, even closer than before! Panting hoarsely, he staggered toward the other side of the knoll.

"No," cried a high-pitched voice overhead. "Come this way!"

"Elf!" Though almost ready to collapse, he followed

the faery across the knoll to a stand of tall, dark spruce trees.

"Over here," she urged, wings buzzing. "You can do it!"

Like a radiant blue torch, she guided him through the thick tangle of spruce branches. Bursting out the other side of the trees, Elf cried, "Come, Shim. It's your only chance!"

Too tired to see where she was leading him, Shim stumbled through the trees—

Over a cliff! He plunged downward, flailing his arms wildly.

Splash!

Coughing and sputtering, he surfaced in a wide lake. Following the luminous faery, he swam weakly toward a small island that rose from the lake's center. Because the sun had now set, ushering in the shadows of dusk, her light shone like a beacon. A beacon meant to guide him across the water.

Just then, the gobsken warriors emerged from the spruce trees, barely able to stand from all their exertion. Seeing Shim trying to swim away, they shouted multiple curses at him. One of them, in sheer frustration, hurled his shield into the water. It splashed down just an arm's length from Shim and promptly sank.

Shim, meanwhile, focused all his willpower on staying afloat. Utterly drained, he felt ready to follow the shield to rest on the bottom . . . but forced himself to paddle weakly toward the island. All the while, Elf flew ahead of him, calling encouragement. He couldn't understand much of what she was saying, with all the water sloshing in his ears, but the sound of her voice helped keep him going.

From the top of the cliff, the gobsken watched in frustration. Helpless to catch the spy, they both knew that they'd never tell their captain about this failed chase. Or else he'd rage at them and probably slice off their hands . . . or heads.

"At least," growled one of the warriors as he stared angrily at the swimmer below, "he'll likely drown before long."

The other gobsken mopped his sweaty brow with the back of his hand. "Or get eaten by some deadly water beast."

"Not much there worth eating," cracked his mate.

Chortling, the other declared, "Let's leave him to die."

With a glance at the dusky sky, he spat, "He'll drown in the dark."

Spinning around, they dived back into the tangle of branches. After taking several angry swipes with their broadswords and splintering some boughs, they vanished from sight.

Shim, now well out into the lake, continued to swim. But it was very rough going. Just taking a breath, let alone lifting his arms out of the water, was a struggle.

Dead tired, he didn't know whether he'd actually make it all the way to the island. Yet he did know, beyond doubt, that his friend Elf remained with him, glowing just ahead as he swam. That he carried a precious crystal in his pocket. And that he'd come too far, endured too much, just to drown in some nameless lake.

And so, with all his will, he kept swimming.

25.

THE ISLAND

At last, Shim touched the island's edge. Though wet and slippery, the land gave him just enough purchase to pull himself out of the lake. Kicking with all his remaining strength, he hauled his limp, bedraggled body onto shore. Even as the sky darkened with nightfall, he knew that he was finally safe.

Elf, glowing like a blue star, landed beside him. Her bells rippled with joyful sounds as she watched her friend relax.

"You made it!" she exclaimed.

Still panting hard, the little giant didn't respond right

away. After a moment, when his breathing returned to something like normal, he slowly sat up. He shook his wet mop of hair, spraying the faery and soaking the shoreline around them.

"Ugh," he groaned. "There's one thing worse than getting shrunkelled."

Elf shook the water off her wings. "What's that?"

"Getting shrunkelled and then almost eaten and then earthquaked and then chased by gobsken and then very nearly drownishded!"

To a merry peal of bells, the faery answered, "You have a point."

She leaped into the air and buzzed up to his face. Looking him right in the eyes, she said, "I'm proud of you, Big Friend."

With two fingers, he tugged at a clump of watermoss that had lodged in his ear. Finally extracting it, he said, "Proud of you, too, Elf."

He tossed the moss aside. "Even if you did try to drownish me."

She landed, chuckling, on his shoulder. "You're too full of hot air to drown."

Feeling almost fully recovered, Shim scanned the

nighttime scene. By now, the first stars had started to appear, and their reflections already sparkled in the surrounding waters. In the stars' silvery light, he scanned the contours of the island. Small and treeless, it sat in the middle of the lake, a true safe harbor.

Turning his gaze to the starry sky overhead, he searched for the familiar shapes of his favorite constellations. There was Pegasus, soaring on high with enormous wings. And there, Gwri of the Golden Hair. And over there, the wondrous shape of Endless Ocean, where islands of stars dotted the dark expanse.

Dark—because in the Fincayran tradition, the constellations weren't made of stars, but the vast spaces between them. The spaces that might, at first, seem empty.

Elf, who was also gazing up at the constellations, chimed harmoniously. Her tone full of wonder, she said, "As far away as the stars are from here, whenever I look at them, I go even farther. For there is no limit, no end, to my imagination."

Shim nodded, then took a good sniff of the night air. Puzzled, he cocked his head. "This place smells strangelyish . . . more like old leather than land." He sniffed again. "And like something else, too, something familiar—but no, that can't possibly be right."

"Who cares what it smells like?" asked the faery. "All that matters is this island saved you from those gobsken."

He shrugged. "You're right about that!" He started to add, *Certainly, definitely, absolutely*—but caught himself.

Surveying the little island, he observed, "Too bad nothing grows here. We could use a bit of food, even just one fruitly tree. And there's no goodly shelter here, either—just those two caves over there. But they look way too dark and windily to enter."

"Sure," Elf replied, "but look at it this way." She waved a glowing wing at the lake that surrounded them. "At least we've got plenty of water."

With a smirk, he said, "I can always count on you for the brightish side."

"That's why I'm a luminous faery."

She started to laugh at her own joke, then stopped. Her radiance dimmed. In a much quieter voice, she added, "The very *last* luminous faery. With no family left—not even my twin sister."

Shim sighed compassionately. "I understand, truly I do." After a few seconds of silence, he went on. "And I'm the very last giant. With no family, no city, no home."

He ran his hand through his wet and scraggly hair. "On top of that, I've lost something else."

Elf peered at him somberly. "What's that?"

"Well . . . I've also lost a bigly part of my memory."

He swallowed. "Which means that I've lost some of myself. The truth is . . . I don't really know who I am."

Suddenly, the island shook violently. Elf shrieked and took flight, while Shim clung tightly to the shore beneath him. The whole island quaked, shifted—then lifted out of the lake!

Higher and higher it rose, carrying Shim upward. It took all his concentration—and all the muscles of his fingers and toes—just to hang on.

Then, in a booming voice, the island beneath him spoke. Though it said only a few words, they carried as much meaning as an entire library.

"You may not know who you are, young giant. But I do."

26.

THE SECRET DOOR

Shim was so shocked by what had just happened—the island suddenly rising out of the lake and the weighty words spoken by that voice—he lost his grip and fell.

Tumbling off the island, he braced himself to land with a splash in the cold water of the lake. He glimpsed, hovering above him, Elf's radiant blue light. She looked like a bright blue jewel set in the midst of the glittering stars of Fincayra's night sky.

At the very instant of impact, he hit—not water, but something soft and supple. Moist with water droplets.

With the same leathery smell that he'd detected on the island. But what was it?

Skin. Cupped all around him. Like a hand.

A giant hand.

"Whoa, wha—but, no! This, but . . ." he stammered, trying to find the right words.

As he sat up, Elf zipped down and perched on his shoulder. Accompanied by some cheerful notes, she teased, "Articulate as always, Big Friend."

Shim ignored her. His attention was directed entirely to the huge, wet face staring down at them, with azure-blue hair and thick, curvy lips. A face he recognized!

Hesitantly, he asked, "Umdahla? Is it really you?"

The giant's curvy lips smiled. "I guess you haven't lost your special way of speaking, Shim."

"What everishly do you mean by that?" he asked. He tried to stand up in her enormous palm, but lost his balance and toppled over, sending the faery back into flight.

The giant peered down at him as he righted himself and sat again, this time leaning against the base of her huge thumb. "But you certainly *have* lost something else. Like . . . ninety-nine percent of your size!"

He merely frowned.

"How did it happen?"

Shim shook his head sadly. "How did I get so utterly shrunkelled? I really don't know." Giving his ear an anxious tug, he said, "I just . . . don't . . . remember."

Umdahla wrinkled her massive brow in concern. "Yet you remember me, right?"

"Surely, I do! You were my neighbor in Varigal. Why, I even remember your smell, yes indeedily! That's why when I smelled the skin of—whatever part of you we thought was an island—I thought it was familiar."

"My nose," the giant replied, lifting her other hand out of the lake to touch the very tip of her nose. "You landed on my nose."

Confused, he squinted up at her. "But you're so underwaterly, how do you breathe?"

She shrugged her gargantuan shoulders, making her blue hair, still wet from the lake, ripple with starlight. "Through my nostrils, of course—those two caves you saw before. Aside from my nose, I'm entirely submerged. Fortunately, this lake is deep enough to cover someone as big as me."

"And as bigly," he added with a frown, "as I used to be."

Elf zipped down and landed again on his shoulder. "But you're still a giant at heart," she reminded him. Turning to face Umdahla, she added, "I can testify to that, I promise you."

Umdahla pursed her lips thoughtfully. "So then what happened to you?"

"I told you alreadily. I just don't remember."

"Yet you remember me, and even my particular smell. And you said you remember Varigal." She paused. "Do you remember your mother, my dear friend Vonya?"

Shim started. That name sounded so very familiar . . . yet, at the same time, cut off from his memory. He could almost recall it—but not quite. Like so much else, it seemed hidden behind an impossibly thick veil.

He rubbed his forehead, trying to recall. It felt like the information was there, somewhere in his mind, but completely shrouded. Behind that veil, he sensed, was a secret door to the room that held all his lost memories . . . but there wasn't any way to find that door, let alone open it.

"No," he answered glumly. "I don't remember."

"Strange," observed Umdahla. "Very strange."

She glanced up at the constellations, as if hoping for

some wise counsel from the stars. Turning back to Shim, she said, "Maybe this will help. You know why I've taken to soaking day and night in this lake, don't you?"

Uncertainly, he replied, "Because you like a good bath?"

She rolled her eyes. "You may have earned your true name—and I was there on that night, watching it happen—but you still have a lot to learn!"

"That's for surely. So why are you here, being so wackily waterish?"

Lowering her face so that her chin nearly touched the hand that held him, she said, "Because I'm *hiding*, Shim! From all the enemies of giants—starting with that wicked Stangmar. His warriors would love to carve me into pieces, just like they did to so many giants that night they invaded Varigal."

He grimaced. "I remember that night, believe me. The most horribobulous night of my life."

Sympathetically, she nodded. "Mine too." Blinking back some tears, she said softly, "Until you came along just now, I thought I was the only giant who survived that night. The only one of all our people, so ancient and bonded to the history of Fincayra, who still lived."

She paused to blink again. "The only way I escaped

was by using the old gate behind Lunahlia's cottage. The attack came so suddenly, without warning . . . the only chance anyone had to survive was to run and hide. Either that or—"

She caught herself, struck by an idea.

"That or what?" both Shim and Elf asked at once.

"*Transform.*" Seeing their bewildered expressions, she explained, "When the attack came, every mother and father wanted desperately to protect their children. That's what Vonya wanted for you, I'm certain."

She took a deep breath. "To protect you during the attack was hard enough. But even if you survived, there was another problem—a truly terrible problem: how to keep you safe afterward, and for the rest of your life. Or at least until Stangmar could be overthrown and giants could live freely again."

"Giants and all the rest of us," the faery added somberly.

"But as long as you still looked like a big, strapping giant, you—"

"Would still be hunted by Stangmar's wickedly warriors," Shim finished grimly. "And we know what that means."

"Right. So you could try to hide—but there are only so many lakes and boulder fields that might work. Or maybe . . . you could transform into something different. Like a bird or a living stone or a sea lion."

Shim's whole body tensed. "Or a teensily little person who nobody would ever suspect is a giant."

Gravely, Umdahla nodded. "There's a big problem with that, though. Transformations require a huge amount of magic. And with the wizardking Tuatha gone, nobody in Fincayra has that much power."

The giant shook her enormous head, causing her wet hair to slap against her shoulders. "I don't know how anyone, even a mother as smart as yours, could have ever gotten you shrunken."

"Shrunkelled," said Shim, correcting her grammar.

She grinned ever so slightly, then looked with grave seriousness at the little fellow in her hand. "I knew Vonya very well . . . and I'm sure she would have thought of getting you transformed. Yet there's nobody alive who could actually do it."

Under her breath, she muttered, "Except maybe Domnu. But that's impossible."

Shim suddenly perked up—as if hearing that name

had broken a single thread in the veil that separated him from his memories. "What was that name again?"

Umdahla shrugged. "Domnu. An ancient hag. A sorceress."

Shim's eyes widened as, deep in his mind, another thread broke. "Whateverly else do you know about her?"

"Well . . . she lives in the Haunted Marsh. That's the deadliest place on this whole island—so frightful that nobody would ever choose to go there."

More threads burst apart. Shim felt himself pulling at the veil deep inside his mind, trying as hard as he could to tear it away. Yet it still held firm, shrouding so much— including the secret door he wanted desperately to open.

"I've heard about that place," said Elf with a shudder. Though Shim could still hear her, the faery's voice sounded more faded and distant than before. "And I've heard that the only other beings who live there are ghouls with haunted, glowing eyes."

Now, inside himself, Shim fought and flailed, pulling against the veil with renewed strength. More threads ripped, revealing a gaping hole. And beyond that, he could almost see a distant shape—something that just might be a door.

"Yes," answered Umdahla, her voice also sounding muffled to Shim. "Just one look into those eyes, they say, will drive anyone mad."

Shim struggled even harder, reaching through the veil. He stretched out his arms, grasping at the door. He could almost touch the latch . . . but just couldn't reach it.

If Elf and Umdahla hadn't been so engrossed in their conversation, they'd have noticed signs of Shim's anguished struggle. His eyes blinked rapidly, while the fingers of both hands twitched frantically.

"I've also heard," continued Elf in her faded voice, "that Domnu's lair is even more terrifying than the ghouls. The whole place is supposed to be surrounded by . . ."

Stretching even farther, pulling hard against the veil, Shim felt his fingertip brush the latch.

"Surrounded by what?" asked Umdahla, her voice still muffled.

Elf hesitated before replying. Deep in his internal struggle, Shim barely heard her say, "By thousands and thousands of . . ."

Shim grabbed the latch at last. He threw open the door and shouted, "Bones! Bones everlywhere!"

Shaking from the strain, he announced, "I was there. Really and truly and scarily, I was!"

Umdahla gasped. Her voice loud and clear again, she exclaimed, "If you were there, then so was your loving—"

"Motherly!"

All at once, Shim remembered everything: The perilous journey with his mother. The ghouls who finally helped them cross the marsh. The precarious pile of stones surrounded by bones. The terrible wager. The horrendous sacrifice his mother made. And last, in painful clarity, Domnu's spell that so brutally smallified him.

As he stared at Umdahla in astonishment, more memories returned. How lovingly his mother embraced him. How proud she looked when he earned his true name. How diligently she tried—and failed—to keep his leggings repaired.

And then one more memory returned, echoing with the sound of her voice. How she urged him to remember: *Bigness means more than the size of your bones.*

Though he remained small in body, Shim felt somehow bigger. As if an important part of himself that had gone missing had suddenly been restored. He stood up, balancing himself in Umdahla's palm. Glancing from her to Elf, who was glowing her brightest blue, he spoke to them with fierce determination.

"We were there. Motherly is still there now. And I am going to go back there to save her."

He paused, then declared, "Certainly, definitely, absolutely!"

27.

THE LAST OF HER KIND

Beneath Fincayra's starry sky, Elf and Umdahla tried their very best to dissuade Shim from his plan. They reminded him that surviving the Haunted Marsh was an absolute miracle, and he'd somehow already done that twice. So he wasn't likely to survive it again. They convinced him that Domnu had hidden his memories of his mother precisely to prevent him from ever trying to come back and rescue her. They told him that he could never outwit Domnu—just as he could never beat her in a wager. On top of all that, they pleaded with him to remember that he wasn't nearly as physically big and strong as he'd once been.

None of it worked. He was absolutely determined to go back for his mother.

As he stood in the hand of Umdahla, he declared, "I want to give her the same greatly devotion she gave to me. You're her friend . . . so you must understand."

The giant drew a long breath of night air and shifted her weight in the lake, which sent star-sparkled waves rolling in all directions. "Here is what I do understand," she replied in her gentlest voice. "That night in Varigal, you really deserved to earn your true name."

"Thanks, Umdahla."

She peered down at him. "But I still think your plan is absolutely foolish, dangerous, and doomed."

He nodded. "Full of madness, that's me."

He turned to the faery who was standing on his shoulder. "I know you don't agree with anyishthing I've said."

"Except for the part about madness," she replied.

"All rightly, except for that. But, Elf . . . can you ever forgive me?"

"No," she stated firmly. "Which is why . . . I'm coming with you."

Shim brightened. "Really and truly?"

The faery bobbed her head, ringing her bells with finality. "As you would say—certainly, definitely, absolutely."

Umdahla shook her massive head. "So you're *both* crazy! And I can see there's no dissuading you."

"You're correctly."

Gazing down at him, she said grimly, "Part of me wants to join you, make no mistake about that. But I'm sure there's just no way for anyone to defeat Domnu—so you and Vonya are certainly going to die. And while I could sacrifice my own life for a great cause . . . I just can't sacrifice the life of *the very last giant alive*. The only one of our people who will remain. The last little connection to all our history, all our stories. Can you understand?"

His expression equally grim, Shim declared, "I understand. And if we don't survive this . . . I hope you will live long enough to share the giants' awesomely stories with the whole wide world."

She studied the brave little giant and the faery on his shoulder. "You remind me of something I haven't thought about for a long time. Something my father once told me."

Both Shim and Elf watched her, intrigued.

"He was a boat builder, Papa. Worked many years to help humans build their fishing boats on the west coast, in the great bay near the Misted Hills. He used to carry the trees they needed for masts and lift them up high so they could ready the sails."

She glanced up at the stars. "Once, when I was very young, he talked about times like this. He said: *On the stormy seas of life, the winds of hope and goodness and love are always blowing. All we need to do is find the courage to go out there . . . and raise our sails.*"

The companions nodded gratefully.

Umdahla then announced, "There is, at least, one way I can still help you."

"What?" asked Shim.

"I can save you another swim."

With that, Umdahla stood up, lifting her immense head and shoulders so high above the surface of the lake that, it seemed to Shim, she could almost brush her hair against the stars. Rising up, she caused rows of waves to splash against the lakeshore. As she stood waist-deep in water, she winked at the passengers riding in her hand.

"I haven't carried you, Shim, since you were a wee newlyborn."

He smirked. "Hope I didn't go poopishly in your hands."

"No," she said with a chuckle, "you didn't." Then in just two giant-size strides, she carried them to the water's edge. Kneeling, she gently set them down on solid ground.

"There," she said kindly. "Now you can get going without delay."

Shim looked up at her with sincere gratitude. Although he stood only as tall as her ankle, he knew beyond any doubt that they belonged to the same people. With his memory—and his identity—finally restored, he felt certain that he was truly a giant. Just a rather little one.

"Thank you, Umdahla, from the bottomishmost part of my heart. You helped me remember why I must do this."

"And thank you, Shim. You helped me remember why I must stay alive."

A gleam in her eyes, she said, "Now I have one more thing to do before you go." Glancing at Elf, she added, "Faery, you should take flight."

Shim shot the giant a puzzled look. What was she going to do?

As Elf lifted off, Umdahla reached out her hand and extended one finger. Very gently, she touched the tip of her finger to each of Shim's shoulders—the traditional Giants' Salute.

The moment she touched him, Shim felt as if his heart had expanded inside his chest. To the size of a heart that belonged to a giant.

"As you know," she declared, "this salute is only for someone who has earned another giant's highest respect."

"I won't everly disappoint you."

She curled her lips in a smile. "There's no way you could, Shim. Now go out and show that sorceress who's boss. And if, by some miracle, you survive . . . come back here and visit me."

"I will, yes indeedily."

Elf landed back on his shoulder, chiming softly. She peered up at Umdahla's face and said, "I am so glad to have met you."

The giant nodded, her azure hair glistening in the starlight. "Yes, little one. It was good to see you again."

The faery started. "Again? What do you mean? We haven't met before."

Umdahla furrowed her brow. "You don't remember?

You came here just two nights ago, very tired. You rested on the island—my nose—until I lifted out of the lake for a chat."

Elf shook her antennae, confused. "Are you sure it wasn't some other faery?"

Taken aback, the giant replied, "Come now! A luminous faery with golden bells? How many of those could there be?"

Elf's whole body blazed bright, casting blue light over them all. "Two! And only two!"

"What?"

"You met my sister. She must still be alive!"

Shim gasped. "Most probobily, she thinks she's the only one left, the last of her kind."

"Right," answered Elf, her joy now mixing with concern. "And I know how hard that can be."

"So do I," agreed Umdahla.

Fluttering up to the giant's face, Elf hovered there. "Tell me. How did she seem?"

"Sad. Very sad."

The faery's radiance dimmed. "Did she say where she was going?"

"No. But she flew off to the west."

Slowly, Elf floated down to hover above Shim's nose. "Big Friend . . ." she started to say, but her voice failed.

He gazed at her knowingly. "You've got to go after her. You indeedily must."

For several heartbeats, she gazed back at him. "You are a true friend."

He made a sad smile and tapped his shoulder where she'd so often perched. "There will always be a place rightly here for you."

Her glowing wings brightened a bit. "I plan to be back there sometime soon. After you save your mother and we meet again."

He swallowed. "I surely hope so."

Suddenly remembering, he pointed at the bulging pocket that held the Leaper. "What do you want to do with this, Elf? It belongs to you."

"No," she said with a firm shake of her bells. "It now belongs to *you*."

"But—"

"You've earned it, Shim." She zipped closer and put her hand on his ear. "And I have a feeling you could use it right now."

Seeing the wisdom in her words, he replied, "You're right."

"Haven't you learned by now?" she teased. "I'm always right."

"Of coursely."

"All right, then," she declared, flying back up to hover in front of him. "Let's both go and find our families."

He nodded at her, this little creature who now had such a big place in his heart. "Till we meet again."

She rang her antennae bells one last time, a sound that wove together joy and sorrow, gain and loss, hope and fear. And then she said softly, "Go now . . . and live with light."

She spun around and flew off to the west, leaving a luminous trail like a shooting star.

As Umdahla watched, fascinated, Shim pulled the magical crystal from his pocket. He closed his eyes, concentrating. Suddenly, the crystal flashed with orange light, so bright that Umdahla had to blink.

When she reopened her eyes, Shim had vanished.

28.

BONES AND STONES

Instantly, Shim found himself in a dreadful, but familiar, place. Giving the magical crystal a squeeze, he whispered, "Thanks." Then he slid it back into his pocket and surveyed his surroundings.

Dark fumes swept around him, smelling like rancid waste and rotting flesh. All around, he heard bubbling mud pits, hissing vents, and in the distance, the menacing shrieks and moans of marsh ghouls.

And there, directly in front of him, rose the haphazard pile of stones that he now remembered well. Domnu's lair.

The towering structure actually looked slightly

sturdier than before. More stones, cut with straight edges and sharp corners, had been stacked carefully around the base. But overall, the structure remained precarious enough to scare away any unwanted visitors. It still deserved Shim's term *ramshackelous*.

As before, the lair's barred windows glowed with eerie, unnatural light. They cast wavering amber rays over the masses and masses of bones piled everywhere. Among those bones, Shim knew, were the remains of many creatures who once lived freely, flying or crawling or walking . . . until they met Domnu.

He shuddered, examining the lair. *Motherly is in there now, a prisoner in that awfullously ominous place!*

Though he knew what he needed to do—the question was how. Maybe he could make use of Domnu's penchant for wagers? He started to form the hazy outline of a plan. Yet just like any wager with the sorceress, the odds of success were extremely small.

He drew a breath of the rancid air. Then, his expression grim, he climbed over a pile of bones, an uprooted tree, and a heap of rubble before finally reaching the entrance to the tunnel that would lead him inside. As before, the dark hole gaped ominously.

Bravely, he stepped into the passageway. The amber light grew stronger as he went deeper. Finally, he reached the heavy door that, this time, sat wide open. As if he'd been expected.

Shim entered the cavernous room supported by immense, rotting beams. Scanning the room, he saw much of what he'd seen before. The hairy rug by the wall with living chess pieces, including the unicorn whose white mane glistened. The rock wall covered with bizarre markings, runes, and numbers, plus a new drawing of a labyrinth. The bowls piled high with jewels, shells, bones, more bones, crystal spheres, cards, and bundles of hair. And, of course, the iron bowl that held nothing but wet, oozing eyeballs.

"Well, well," growled a familiar voice. "A visitor. How very . . . unexpected."

Shim whirled around to see the sorceress emerge from the shadows. Her eyes, black and unblinking, gazed at him malevolently. All the while, she toyed with her necklace—this one made from the skulls of mice and snakes.

As soon as she stepped into the light, the unicorn chess piece made a sound like a strangled neigh. Domnu, without taking her eyes off Shim, pointed at the unicorn, and the creature instantly fell silent. But her deep brown eyes continued to shift frantically.

Domnu approached slowly and steadily, much like a predator who was preparing to pounce on her prey. Passing a hand over her wrinkled scalp and the wart that protruded from her forehead, she examined the little giant closely. Her gaze rested briefly on the bulging pocket of his leggings.

"Now tell me," she growled. "What brings you here?"

Scowling, Shim replied, "You mean, actuallishly, what brings me *back* here."

Domnu, clearly surprised, furrowed her brow. "So you remember your last visit?"

"I remember," he declared, straightening his small back. "And I've come back for Motherly."

Domnu's furrows deepened. "I must say, my pet, you are more resilient than I expected. So I'm glad that I left my door open."

Carelessly, she flicked a finger at the oaken door. It slammed shut with a boom that echoed around the chamber.

Though the slam made him start, and his heart pounded inside his chest, Shim did his best to appear calm. He glanced around the room for any evidence of his mother—even a stray lock of her scraggly hair. But he saw no sign of her.

Domnu chortled knowingly. "Your mother is downstairs, working on today's task. Cleaning out my dungeons—something that's several centuries overdue."

Seeing Shim perk up, she added nonchalantly, "She's a decent worker . . . for a witless servant."

He grimaced. "I'm not here, you crumbumbly old crone, to waste time talking. I'm here to offer you a wager."

Domnu perked up. "What sort of wager, my pet?"

"For something of greatly value."

She scratched her wart. "Not you, that's for sure. You're too smallified to be any use . . . and too rebellious, as well. It's in your blood. Your mother caused me plenty of trouble, believe me, before I finally *persuaded* her to stop."

She grinned maliciously, showing a mouthful of misshapen teeth. "A certain amount of pain, applied in just the right places, can tame even the most rebellious servant."

Shim bristled, but tried hard to stay focused. "Are you going to wager or not?"

She shrugged, causing whatever objects were hidden in the pockets of her robe to clatter. "I don't see what you could have that would be worth the trouble to wager."

"Really?" He reached into his pocket and pulled out the Leaper. "What about this?"

Despite herself, Domnu quivered with excitement as she stared at the orange crystal. "Well, well, my pet. You are full of surprises."

Watching her, Shim felt a sudden wave of doubts. Had he betrayed the crystal by bringing it into the lair of this evil sorceress? Did that make him no longer true of heart? How could he possibly prevail?

Domnu, meanwhile, contained her eagerness and put on a calm demeanor. "Of course, you realize that I could just take that crystal from you right now. That is, if I really wanted it."

"Sure," Shim replied. "But what would be anyish fun about that? Wouldn't you much rather win it, fairly and squarely, in a wager?"

"Yes," she replied, cracking her withered knuckles with glee. "The anticipation is the best part, even though I always know from the start that I'm going to win."

Quickly, she corrected herself. "Though a wager is a wager, so there is always a chance I could lose. And of course, my pet, I would *never* cheat."

"Never," he agreed. He nodded emphatically—even though he remembered quite clearly how she had cheated his mother.

"Well, then," growled the hag, "what shall be the stakes?"

Over by the wall, the spellbound unicorn's eyes shifted fearfully. She released the barest whisper of a neigh.

"The stakes," declared Shim, "are verily simple. If I win—"

"No! Stop!" boomed a powerful voice from across the room.

"Motherly!"

Seeing his beloved mother emerge from the dungeons, climbing up through a trapdoor, Shim started to run over to embrace her. But Domnu stepped right in front of him and raised a hand.

"One more step," she snarled, "and I will turn both of you into worms and cast you into the Haunted Marsh." Under her breath, she added, "As I should have done when you first arrived."

Shim halted . . . but that took all his willpower. His heart felt ready to burst. Yet he knew he'd have just one chance to free his mother—and that would be hard enough to accomplish in their current forms, let alone as a pair of worms. So he complied . . . even as he shot his mother a soulful gaze. A gaze she returned.

Pivoting to face Vonya, the sorceress barked, "Bad timing, you imbecile. We were just about to set the terms of a wager!"

Before Vonya could reply, Domnu stretched out both her arms and sent out a blast of air-crackling energy. Instantly, the giant was lifted out of the trapdoor and thrown brutally against the stones of one wall. The entire lair shook with the impact, knocking down the remains of a rotted beam that crashed to the floor behind Shim.

Simultaneously, heavy shackles appeared on the wall and wrapped themselves around Vonya's arms and legs. The shackles' chains, whose links were as thick as the giant's own wrists, sprouted right out of the stones.

Shim gasped, horrified to see her treated like that. His own mother—chained to the wall! He boiled with outrage. Yet he knew that, for now, he could do nothing . . . and that made him boil even more.

"No!" shouted Vonya as she twisted violently, trying to break her bonds. But they held fast.

Domnu, watching her struggle, grunted in satisfaction. Then she muttered, "Just one more detail, my pet."

The sorceress flicked her finger. Instantly, a sturdy gag tied itself around Vonya's jaw, making it impossible for her to speak. All she could do now was moan wretchedly, a sound that pierced Shim's heart like a dagger.

Indifferent to the heartrending moans, Domnu turned back to him. "There, my pet. Where were we?"

Though his eyes darted anxiously toward his mother, he steeled himself and returned to the task at hand. Mustering all his focus, he answered Domnu's question.

"The stakes. If I win," he said with a wave at his mother, still struggling unsuccessfully with the shackles, "then she and I both go free! Not as worms or anyish otherly beings, but as ourselves."

Domnu gave a nod of agreement.

"And no tricksyness, none at all."

Again, she nodded. "And if I win?"

Shim inhaled slowly. "If you win . . . you can take this magical crystal." Hefting the Leaper, he turned it so its facets sparkled with the promise of dazzling power.

"Very tempting," growled the sorceress. "I don't know that particular crystal . . . though I can tell it might have a small amount of power. So then, after I win and take it for my own, what will happen to you?"

From the wall, Vonya's moans rose into a howl of protest. Why had she given up her freedom, only to see her son destroyed by this horrible hag? She tugged harder than ever on her shackles—but to no avail.

Shim swallowed. "Then you can do whatever you like with me."

Domnu cackled. "As you wish, my pet."

Sliding the crystal back into his pocket, the little giant declared, "Let's do this." Glumly, he added, "And I suppose we should use bones, the same as you used to wager Motherly. If I'm going to lose . . . I'd like to lose the same way she did."

The sorceress flashed her twisted teeth. "How sweetly sentimental of you."

She snapped her fingers. As before, a ceramic vase appeared, floating between them. From its mouth protruded five thin bones.

In a naive tone of voice, Shim asked, "How does this go? Can you remind me?"

"You weren't paying attention last time, I guess. No surprise, since you were writhing in pain." Pleased by the thought, she snickered cheerfully.

"All right, then." She pointed at the bones. "Whoever

chooses the tallest one wins. Here are your choices."

As she indicated each bone, an invisible bell rang out, echoing in the cavernous space around them. Just as Shim had noticed before, the notes varied— and at the lowest note, the sorceress grinned almost imperceptibly.

In the background, Vonya's howls grew louder. She pulled on her bonds with all her might, straining with effort. But the shackles, anchored in the stones behind her, held firm.

Yet . . . something shifted. Vonya felt the slightest little movement in her bonds—but it wasn't from any weakening of her chains. So what could it be?

In a flash, she realized. *The stones.* She threw herself into pulling harder, using every fiber in her body.

Shim, meanwhile, saw his moment of opportunity. Swiftly, he reached for the bone that had been accompanied by the lowest note. He pulled it out of the vase—and gasped.

The bone was short! Barely half as tall as the vase, it clinked against the rim as he pulled it free.

"How disappointing," clucked Domnu as she pulled out a much larger bone. "Too bad, my pet."

Her expression abruptly turned vengeful. "You didn't really expect me to fall for your pathetic ruse, did you? If so, you're just as stupid as you are small."

Leaning closer, she said, "But you'll soon be even smaller, as a worm."

Unnoticed by anyone, the unicorn chess piece moved her tail the slightest little bit. Determined to break free of Domnu's spell, she quivered all over, trying to unfreeze herself.

Utterly dejected, Shim hung his head. How could he have been so foolish? Of course she'd remember her own trick, and expect him to try to use it against her! And now that his plan had failed, both he and Motherly were truly vanquished.

Unless . . .

His mind raced. There was still one chance left—and only one—to outwit the sorceress. But that chance was terribly slim. It could easily go wrong . . . and would need all his concentration to go right.

"You're rightly," he said in a meek tone of voice. "It was stupid of me, horribobulously stupid, to think that a lowly person like me could ever trick somelyone as geniusish as you."

Domnu clucked with satisfaction. "Maybe you could still prove useful to me." Stroking her scalp thoughtfully, she continued, "Which is why I've changed my mind. Instead of wormifying you . . . I'm going to give you a job."

"A job?"

"Oh yes, a lovely one." Lowering her voice to a snarl, she said, "You will serve as your mother's commander."

He froze.

Warming to her idea, Domnu continued, "If you refuse, then she will die." With a menacing show of teeth, she added, "Of course, she will die anyway. Because *you* will work her to death."

Shim seethed with anger. Yet he held his tongue. For he knew that for his new plan to work, he had to play along and seem hopeless, so as not to rouse her suspicions.

All the while, Vonya pulled mightily on her bonds. One stone behind her back shifted slightly, grinding against the stones above and below. Yet that wasn't nearly enough progress—she needed to do more to save her son. Or die trying!

Meanwhile, Shim continued to look totally dejected.

Which was exactly how he would really feel if this last, desperate ploy didn't succeed.

With a shaking hand, he reached into his pocket and started to pull out the crystal. Beads of sweat moistened his brow. Did he have the right plan? And did he have the right words to pull it off?

Domnu watched him, licking her lips with anticipation.

His hand wrapped around the crystal. *Steadily, now.* Just then, out of the corner of his eye, he caught a glimpse of movement. The unicorn, valiantly trying to break the spell, swished her tail!

He clenched his jaw. If the unicorn could show such courage—well then, by the beard of Dagda, so could he.

Domnu, getting impatient, stretched out her hand. "Give me that thing. No more delay!"

Shim closed his eyes. *Now, Leaper. Take Motherly and me far away from here! Not just so we can survive—but so there will still be somely giants left in this world.*

"Treachery!" shouted Domnu, sensing the magic rising in the crystal. She pointed her hands at Shim, ready to blast him to nothingness, when—

Crash!

Vonya pulled several stones from the wall, destabilizing the wall itself. Dozens of immense stones came smashing down, bursting beams and exploding on the floor. The entire lair started to collapse.

Even as the whole place caved in, Shim added one more request to the glowing crystal in his hand: *And somely unicorns, too.*

There was a sudden flash of orange light.

Domnu shrieked wildly as stones crashed down on top of her, smashing bones, bowls, and all her treasures—including eyeballs. The lair collapsed with such force that powerful tremors shook the entire Haunted Marsh. A dust cloud rose so high that it was seen many leagues away by the poet Cairpré in the Town of the Bards.

Of course, even such a terrible disaster couldn't kill Domnu. She possessed too much power to be destroyed so easily. And for her, the task of rebuilding her lair wouldn't be too difficult. It would, actually, give her the opportunity to make some much-needed improvements—such as expanding her dungeons to leave plenty of room for giants.

No, as she crawled out of the enormous pile of rubble that had so recently been her home, only one fact annoyed her. *Greatly* annoyed her. She knew, through her insight as a sorceress, that three of her most valuable prisoners had somehow escaped.

Domnu rose to her feet, then cursed and stomped so vehemently that even the marsh ghouls shuddered with fear. All the plants that grew on the edges of the marsh suddenly withered and died. The shadowy gloom of the swamp darkened more than ever. And the moon itself felt Domnu's terrible wrath, causing it to hide behind clouds for the next seven days.

29.

ALL THE LIGHT

As the orange light faded, Shim found himself standing on the shore of Umdahla's lake—exactly at the spot where he'd left for Domnu's lair. As before, the dark of night surrounded him, while Fincayra's stars sparkled overhead. He realized that, since he hadn't specified any location, the Leaper had returned him there. Squeezing the crystal gratefully, he slid it back into his pocket.

At that very instant, he heard, right behind him, the sound of shoreline rocks being crushed by something very heavy. He spun around to see an enormous figure kneeling down, opening her arms to embrace him.

"Motherly!"

"Hello, my jelly roll."

They hugged each other for a long time, listening to each other's familiar breathing. Starlight illuminated the paths of joyful tears on their cheeks, as a gentle night breeze tousled their hair.

At last, they pulled apart and simply looked at one another. Vonya examined her son with the keen eyes of a mother. And Shim watched her with the certainty that he had regained everything that he had, for a time, lost.

"I'm guessing," Vonya said quietly, "you've had a few adventures since I last saw you."

"Oh, just a few," he replied.

"Well then, I have a very important question."

"What?"

"Did you rip your britches?"

Both of them burst out laughing.

Just then, Shim felt something nudge his shoulder. Turning, he saw the unicorn gazing at him with her deep brown eyes. No longer spellbound as a chess piece, she stood regally before him. Though she didn't speak a word, Shim felt her send him a sudden rush of gratitude.

The unicorn's horn, which she'd used to nudge him, gleamed wondrously in the light of the stars. Her silver coat, like her long white mane, glistened as if made from the luminous rays on high. She whinnied, stamped her silver hoof on the rocks, then turned and galloped off.

Shim, as well as his mother, watched her depart, hooves clattering. The unicorn's horn continued to gleam until, finally, it was swallowed by the night.

Vonya sighed. Facing her son again, she frowned and said, "I hope you know . . . what I did to you, having you made so small, was—"

"To save me," finished Shim. "I know, Motherly. You were only trying to keep me safe."

Her frown melted away. "And how are you feeling about that?"

"Well . . . it took me a while, wandering clumsyishly around Fincayra, to get used to it. And the hardest part, by far, was not remembering *you*."

Vonya grimaced. "That was a terrible thing for Domnu to do."

"It was. But together, we're more strongly than any spell."

"Yes, we are."

"And now," Shim continued, "I know that I'm still a giant. Just . . . a giant of a differentish size."

Leaning forward, Vonya hugged him again. "You, my son, are the biggest giant I have ever known."

When she released him, she asked, "What was that crystal you had at Domnu's lair?"

Pulling it out of his pocket, he held it between them, watching its facets shimmer and sparkle. "It's the Leaper. One of the preciously Treasures of Fincayra. And its magic is so strong that it carried us, heartbeatly quick, all the way from the lair to here."

"May I touch it?"

"Of coursely." He dropped the orange crystal into her open palm. "See how it shines so bright when it's held by you? That's because you are somelybody who is true of heart."

She smiled at him, then went back to studying the radiant crystal. "It really does glow with its own light."

Tenderly, Shim placed his hand on the knuckle of her thumb. When she looked over at him, he met her gaze.

"Motherly. I want you to keep it."

"What?" she asked in surprise. "No, Shim—it's yours. You earned it, I'm very sure of that. It belongs to you."

"Well," he said decisively, "I'm giving it to you."

"No." She winked at him. "I've got all the light I need with you around."

He shook his head, then spoke earnestly. "Listen to me, now. It's not safe out there." He waved his arm at the lake and beyond, toward the hills that hid Stangmar's ever-spinning castle. "A giant who really *looks* like a giant is in constant danger."

"You're right," she said grimly. "That's what started this whole thing. You, at least, can now live safely. But I—I will need to hide. At least until Stangmar is no longer ruling Fincayra."

She looked at him worriedly. "After what you've seen in your travels . . . do you believe that prophecy, the Dance of the Giants? The one that says we will someday rise again and destroy his castle?"

"I do." Shim's eyes shone bright. "We will be there, too. We surely will!"

She nodded in agreement.

"But until then, we must keep this crystal, and any otherly Treasures, away from Stangmar."

"Agreed. Nothing's more important than that."

Shim gazed at the distant hills. He knew that,

somewhere out there, were many other good and caring people who loved this island and would fight to save it. Starting with Elf, his brave little friend whose company he sorely missed. And who would always have her special perch on his shoulder.

Other names, too, came to him. The greathawk Rowallon, whose round eyes glowed with gratitude. The woodswoman Rhia, who could speak with all the creatures in her enchanted forest. And of course, the wise woman Olwen, who could see far beyond her secret chamber in the waterfall.

With a sudden jolt, he realized what Olwen had meant about his true quest. Regaining the Leaper had been only part of it. And maybe saving his mother, as vital as that was, didn't finish it.

Shim drew a deep breath. Was it possible that he might still accomplish some other things? Maybe even some giant-size things?

Turning back to Vonya, he pointed at the crystal in her hand. "Keep it safe. And use it if you everly need to escape from those wickedly warriors."

Her eyes misty, she nodded. "Only if I can also use it sometimes to visit you."

Putting his hands on his hips, he declared, "You better!"

She grinned sadly. "All right, then. Will you show me how the magic works?"

"Of coursely. And I'm guessing you'll get it more quickishly than I did."

She hefted the crystal. "Don't be too sure about that, my jelly roll."

Shim glanced at the lake, whose water sparkled in the starlight. Seeing the small, treeless island in its center, he turned back to his mother.

"First, though, you need to give me a littlish ride. Out to that island. There's somelybody there you need to see."

"Whatever you say, you great big giant."

Scooping up Shim, Vonya stepped into the lake. Ripples rolled across the starlit water, glittering all around them. It looked as if they were moving among galaxies, striding on the very firmament of the stars.

SOME TIME LATER...

S him crossed a small, moss-banked stream on the out-skirts of Druma Wood. Abruptly, he stopped. Right in front of him, in the middle of a glade filled with sprawling megafern, sat one of his most cherished sights.

A broken tree trunk that oozed, from every knothole, wildflower honey.

Smacking his lips hungrily, he stepped slowly closer, all his senses alert for honeybees. But he didn't hear, see, or smell any sign of them.

Goodly, he reassured himself. The bees must be off somewhere else. Maybe chasing an unlucky bear who had dared to reach into their precious honey tree. So they won't mind if I take a more closelyish look.

Climbing up to the jagged top of the trunk wasn't easy for his little limbs. Yet he had a strong incentive, and no mere tree trunk was going to keep him away from his most favorite food. A few minutes later, he stood atop the rim, sporting a satisfied grin.

Directly below him lay a golden pool of honey, enough to fill the entire trunk. Surrounded by thick layers of honeycomb, the pool glistened temptingly in the misty light. Within it floated broken bits of bark as well as chunks of honeycomb.

Leaning closer, Shim plunged his hand into the gooey syrup. He took the very first lick—and his eyes opened wide in delight. Such sweetness, such ecstasy!

As honey dripped down his chin, he reached in again for another helping. This time, he leaned even closer, hoping to grab a piece of honeycomb. Just when his fingers touched the pool—

He heard a loud snap!

The rim beneath him ruptured. He shouted and fell right into the pool. Thick, gooey honey covered him completely.

That is the end of this story . . . and the beginning of another one.

Certainly, definitely, absolutely.

Looking for more adventure?
Read the rest of the Merlin Saga, starting with

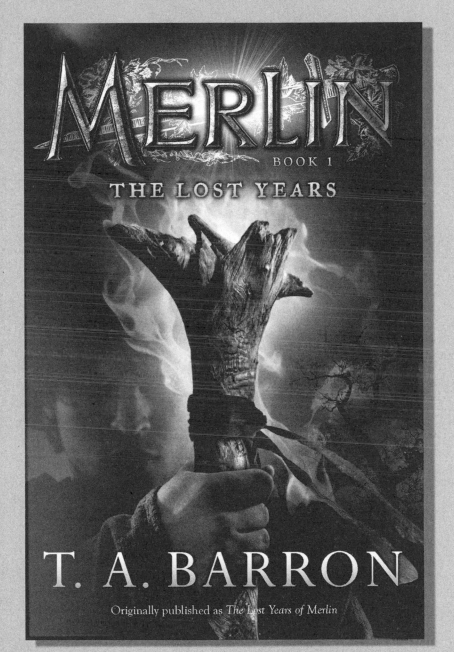

Enter the world of Fincayra in

MERLIN
BOOK 1
THE LOST YEARS

T. A. BARRON

Originally published as The Lost Years of Merlin

MERLIN
BOOK 2
THE SEVEN SONGS

T. A. BARRON

Originally published as The Seven Songs of Merlin

MERLIN
BOOK 3
THE RAGING FIRES

T. A. BARRON

Originally published as The Fires of Merlin

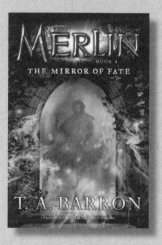

MERLIN
BOOK 4
THE MIRROR OF FATE

T. A. BARRON

Originally published as The Mirror of Merlin

MERLIN
BOOK 5
A WIZARD'S WINGS

T. A. BARRON

Originally published as The Wings of Merlin

MERLIN
BOOK 6
THE DRAGON OF AVALON

T. A. BARRON

Originally published as Merlin's Dragon

MERLIN
BOOK 7
DOOMRAGA'S REVENGE

T. A. BARRON

Originally published as Merlin's Dragon: Doomraga's Revenge

MERLIN
BOOK 8
ULTIMATE MAGIC

T. A. BARRON

Originally published as Merlin's Dragon: Ultimate Magic

MERLIN
BOOK 9
THE GREAT TREE OF AVALON

T. A. BARRON

Originally published as The Great Tree of Avalon: Child of the Dark Prophecy

THE MERLIN SAGA